Music rippled and crashed through Carmen's brain. Opera, her favorite.

She pulled out an earbud, listening for the train. No rumble yet. She reached for her wristwatch, always there. But today, it wasn't. Just as well.

Fingers buried again in pockets, she listened. She had been spoon fed opera since birth, even named after an opera character. It was how she had started. It was how she would end.

The opera blocked out thought and guilt. It frightened away the maggot of self-loathing that fed on Carmen's heart.

In the train's blackened cave, a warning tingle snaked up her legs. It was coming.

She cranked the volume, then curled her fingers around the ledge dividing bored passengers from gleaming metal track.

She let the music's throb boost her gently onto the ledge. She balanced there easily. Busy with books and bytes, no one around her noticed. Carmen's face burned cold.

As the train exploded into view, she began to rock back and forth, merging with the voice pouring into her ears. It was her favorite aria; the clown with the broken heart, pretending to be glad.

Lights blazed ahead, smacked her eyes. The train was here, finally.

It thundered at her. She gave one tiny push forward and let go. Hands reached out, too late.

Then there was music. Cold. Flight.

Nothing.

Song Angel

Nancy Hundal

For Scott, with love,

and for Frances Norman
and *her* song angels,
The Norman Singers

Acknowledgements

With grateful thanks to Linda Bailey and Ardella Thompson for their generous help with this manuscript.

Chapter 1

Blossoms pink as bubblegum drifted over the old woman's tufty hair. They settled on the wattled skin of her arms, on the battered slippers half-buried in spring's sweet grass. At times, she swatted them impatiently from where they landed on the quilt she sewed; at others, she let her head drift back against the chair, feeling them make their laughing way across her withered cheeks.

From the window ledge in the church tower where Carmen watched, the music was so faint that it sounded like memory. But she knew the old woman could hear it. Sometimes the hand holding the needle paused in the air over the quilt, and she angled her head toward her cottage door, from where the music floated.

Gripped tight around the ledge, Carmen's fingers ached. These heights still bothered her, although in another way, the bird-and-sky part of this job was elation. Carefully, she uncurled one hand at a time, wiggling the fingers and her heavy shoulders, then replaced each hand. Only then did she look down again.

The quilt splayed across the woman's lap was a circus of color. From where Carmen watched, it was like miniaturized farm fields through an airplane window, neat rectangles of one color stitched to the next.

The thought of an airplane caught at Carmen's breath; like many other things, her airplane days were over. A lonely cry from above lifted her eyes upward, where a single bird wheeled and tumbled in the breeze. It was heavenly here. Just a little warm, just a little windy, and high up enough that everything on Before seemed perfect. If only she could see the quilt a bit better. She did, after all, have work to do.

Bong! Bong!

The sound crashed in her ears, her bones, her skull.

Bong! Bong!

The shock of it loosed her fingers. Instinct made her push away from the source... anything to free herself from that soul-rattling reverberation. She fell forward, away from the church bell, into the waiting air.

At first, forgetting, her throat opened and a cry almost escaped her. Then she felt the air pull into the pockets behind her shoulders, thrusting her wings outward. Instantly they caught the wind, and Carmen remembered that she'd never have to fall again. She pulsed them wide, loving the power to guide the wispy feathers and sinewy muscles.

And once more, the unbelievable thought floated into her brain...*I am an angel. I, Carmen Michaelson, am a flying-in-the-air, halo-over-head, gossiping-with-God angel.* She twisted a little in the air so she could see the wings from the corner of her eye. She caught a glimpse, but then her body pulled the wings out of sight behind her. Suddenly she knew what a cat chasing its tail felt like. But there must be a way, if you just twisted your head really fast and kind of snuck up on the wings, then...

Forgetting the old woman altogether, Carmen twirled in the air, twisting her head up, down, peeking between her legs, anything to glimpse those wings in action. The woman glanced up, feeling a whorl of energy over her head. Seeing nothing, she went back to her quilt.

"Drat!" Carmen mumbled. "Never get to see these things. Mirrors don't work, can't see back far enough without breaking my angelic neck..."

"Carmen!" Ooooh. There was the voice again, like maple syrup laced with chili peppers. Carmen ceased to twirl, a washing machine agitator slowly losing its spin.

"Um...yes, Zeke?" She could almost see the stern but kindly face, with an expression of...well, the kind of expression an angel commander would have when he sent a recruit off on an angelic mission, only to find her practicing mid-air pirouettes directly above the Electus.

To forestall another of those patient-for-now lectures, Carmen saluted quickly, thankful that there was no real halo to get in her way. She made sure that her lifechain was settled correctly around her neck. "Sorry about that!" She let herself drop gently to the ground. "I'll get on it."

"Yes. Excellent idea." That was all he said. How could he manage to make those three words sound like the strictest principal's warning and a grandmother's coo, all at the same time?

Then the voice was gone, and the feeling in her head that she had company was gone too. Would she ever get used to that? Would the day come when the fact that Zeke had his own channel in her brain seem normal?

A rolling snore pulled her away from brain channels and back to her Electus. Carmen knew her name was Marion. Her head had tipped to one side, hands were folded in her lap, her eyes had closed. Her time in First Life was nearing an end, and she was tired, Carmen knew. She watched the old woman from a distance for a moment, until the bright colors of the quilt drew her eyes downward. Then she tiptoed in for a closer look, never quite convinced that she was invisible to humans.

The quilt was strips of flaming red beside rainbow polka dots, and a chocolaty brown beside a piece of tiny pastel handprints. The patterns and colors seemed endless and random; it wasn't like other quilts Carmen knew of, with many fabrics but an overall plan and color scheme. This one's glory lay in its rambling quality. Like a long story unfolding, it spun itself out from start to finish with a beautiful meander in between.

There was one swatch of fabric: a rich purple combined with velvety green, and a shimmering of something gold through it. Carmen had seen that before. Slowly she closed her eyes, trying to remember. And before she could stop it, her mind became a dark, echoing hallway. She forgot her Electus, the job she'd been sent to do, even Zeke. So many doors! Where was she? What was this place?

But that one door was open, just a crack, so she moved toward it. From inside the door she could feel a pull, like someone holding a fishing rod, reeling her in from the hook caught in her flesh. Then she heard music, two male voices swooping and ducking around each other until they crested on two notes, soaring together. The music became the fishing line, pulling her in, tugging at her heart and her memory. What *was* that music? Where was it taking her? Carmen's body ached to slip past the door.

No. Carmen stepped back from the door and, opening her eyes, felt the door close, the hallway fade. *I don't need to be there. Where I am, this is enough.* She concentrated on the warmish air and the smell of earth in her nostrils until the men's voices bled completely away. She was careful to avoid looking at that elegantly-colored fabric. Best not to go there again. Wherever "there" was.

Beside her, the woman was stirring. She found the needle that had dropped in her lap and resumed her patient stitching. Then she stopped again, looking toward her cottage. Carmen realized then that the music had stopped. It had stopped at the exact moment that the men's melody had ceased in that hallway...could it have been the same song?

"Ah, time to go in," the woman murmured. "My opera is done."

Opera, opera. Carmen knew that word. She could go inside the cottage – she was an angel, she could go anywhere! – but she decided against it. The woman had been listening to opera; that was discovery enough for one day.

Carmen lifted her eyes and the tips of her wings toward the clouds, breaking free of Before and its memories.

Chapter 2

Her body hardly registered the shift into Mezzo. Her thoughts flitted briefly to her very first entry into this world, so long ago now. Or did it just seem so? Time, like everything else, was different in Mezzo.

As she drifted through the now-familiar, Carmen tried to scan her memory for early impressions of Mezzo, before it was home. It seemed as if she'd always been here. But like all the other song angels, she knew she'd lived on Before and had a whole brain file of information on how First Lifes moved, laughed, fought, celebrated and ate...the strangest one of all.

She wasn't sure how she knew about Before; was it from her own life there, or from her work with the Electi, or from the FLims - First Life Films - or all three? She only knew that nothing on Before surprised her, even though she could recall nothing of her own time there.

Well, almost nothing surprised here there. Nothing except eating. Carmen still marveled at the idea of placing objects inside your mouth, moving your lips and teeth up, down and around, then forcing the objects farther into your body...and liking it! That one escaped her. She had a nasty habit of watching, bug-eyed, whenever she caught a First Life eating. Not very angelic, but as Zeke kept reminding her, she was still an angel-work-in-progress.

Carmen could still sense the rumpled feeling from hearing that music, from opening that mind door when she was with her Electus. It gave her the creeps. If she wasn't mistaken, this was her very first real memory from First Life: that music, and the feelings that went with it. Her head felt messy and sore, but at the same time, a little part of her wanted to wiggle back there and hear more, fling that door open and see who or what was inside. There was a nasty sense of inevitability about it, as if a tsunami of memories was roaring toward her. She had resolutely turned her back on it, hoping it would just go away if she ignored it. But that little part wanted to turn and run into it like a maniac, letting the memories trickle over every part of her body and mind.

"Carmen. Welcome back." ChannelZeke was playing again. Carmen liked Zeke – he was, as near as she could tell, a perfect song angel, no doubt one of God's right-hand-angels – but he always had... suggestions. More than suggestions, really.

"Would it be beneficial for you to spend some time in MindSupply?" came the silky voice. Not silky in a bad way, like the handsome-but-evil character in a First Life movie silky. His was more like I-know-what's-best-but-I-know-how-irritating-that-can-be-for-you silky.

"You're not the boss of me!" just wouldn't cut it, for two reasons. Reason Number One: it was a song angel's purpose to learn about the reason they were in Mezzo, when the time was right, and Zeke knew a lot about how to do that. Reason Number Two: he *was* the boss of her. So...

"Yup, Zeke. Here I go," Carmen said. She still spoke aloud to Zeke, although she occasionally wondered if ChannelZeke allowed them both to speak to each other without words.

She hoped not.

Most of Mezzo life she loved, but this cramming two people inside one head – hers! – was not comfortable, and she did all she could to keep ChannelZeke to a minimum. She didn't think he could actually see or hear her thoughts, but she wasn't entirely sure. She'd had many bizarre thoughts since coming to Mezzo, and she was pretty sure that Zeke would have commented by now if he had keyholes into her whole mind. She wasn't sure if speaking aloud to him instead of communicating with thoughts kept him that little bit removed, but it couldn't hurt.

The glowing blues and greens, shining metallics of Mezzo flowed past Carmen as she glided toward MindSupply. If she had to pick one word to describe this place, she'd go with serene. Here, there were places to go, of course – the hammocks for sleep, MindSupply, the grooming chambers, and the Fountain were just a few of the places – but Mezzo wasn't just locations, like First Life. It was a solid space, but also a liquid space, an air space, all flowing together in a calming, luminescent whole. The edges between what you heard and what you saw or felt were blurry and indistinct; you couldn't feel the hard edge of everything here as you could in First Life.

And the music which tumbled everywhere, all the time. Carmen could hear it, feel it, see it. It was a thundering orchestra crashing into children's voices singing the ABC song, then blending to the wail and beckon of a bagpipe. It had taken Carmen time to adjust to this musical backdrop; she had felt every song intensely at first, felt the sudden shift into another tempo or style. She'd been jumbled and headachy all the time from background music that, to her, wasn't in the background.

Gradually, she'd adjusted to the gleam and trill that was Mezzo, as she'd learned to focus on her work as a song angel. Sometimes Carmen wondered if Mezzo was in her mind, or if it was her mind that was in Mezzo. Either way, it was where she lived now. Her song angel work and this wondrous new home made music in her heart, like her melody-filled surroundings.

So why can't I just forget about my First Life… why do I have to remember anything? she groused to herself. *I'm just gonna forget all about that door, and that music!* She felt angel steam rising in her ears and tried to flounce toward MindSupply.

Okay, okay. Flouncing's hard with wings. Feel like I'm doing the bunny hop.

MindSupply wasn't busy. Only a couple of platforms were occupied and, as usual, Dulcie was hooked up on one of them. As Carmen passed by her, she touched Dulcie's wing gently, noting that her wings were even more patchy than Carmen's own. Song angels were a work-in-progress in many ways. Their wings were just one example. Carmen's had at first been pink flesh with a mottled dusting of feathers. Although still nowhere near like Zeke's – ripply with muscle, soft with feather – they were improving.

Dulcie has been here a long time…longer than me, anyway. And her wings never seem to fill in at all, or grow stronger, Carmen mused. She smiled at her friend as she moved onto her own platform, but the smile she got back was a MindSupply smile… only half there, dreamy and absent. It was a smile Carmen saw often on Dulcie's face, even when she wasn't hooked up.

But Carmen needed to move on or Zeke would be tuning in with a focus reminder, so she settled on her own platform. She looked up to watch a jet trail of silver glide toward her; it stopped at her forehead, and she felt the band encircle her skull – all so hi tech, this! Then she waited for her very favorite part. Soon, the two green circles materialized over her eyes, pressing in slowly but insistently, connecting with her mind. Just before her thoughts crystallized elsewhere, there was the usual giggly moment where she imagined a First Life woman, face swathed in cold cream, hair in a towel, slices of green cucumber pressing onto her eyes.

I need to find out about opera. Which she did, but hopefully if she dove right into the research for her Electus, she would also avoid the possibility of getting information she didn't want about that song, where she'd heard it, and what it meant to her other life.

That was the thing about MindSupply – it gave you what you needed most. If that was musical information for your Electus, you got that, or if you were weary or restless, there would be funny or wondrous or educational FLims about life on Before. But MindSupply also somehow sensed what song angels needed to know about their own First Life, usually before they did.

Dulcie said learning about your First Life was like a curtain parting, slowly, slowly, showing you one little section of the play on stage at a time. Dulcie knew most of her story, and was now working with it; Carmen's existence on First Life was still a mystery to her, and that suited her just fine. She knew that only by working through that life could she ever get to the Sweet Hereafter, but it turned out she didn't really care, so what was the rush? No stage crew needed for Carmen. Just keep those curtains closed!

Ooooh...glad I didn't say that out loud. Zeke doesn't need to hear that.

So she eased back against the cushioned platform, glad to rest her shoulders and wings after the exertion of flight. She thought *opera,* then let the little green "cucumbers" do their work. MindSupply played dozens of FLims for her. She learned about arias, songs sung by a main character to highlight their feelings. She heard songs sung adagio, slowly, and sung allegro, quickly. She collected duets and quartets, songs sung by two and four singers. When she learned that male singers were called basses or baritones if they had lower or higher voices, she picked songs with each voice. Women's voices were classified too, so she picked soprano singers, some pitched so high they seemed like a dog whistle! She also found some alto and tenor voices, much lower and more comfortable for Carmen's ears. Amongst the ornate costumes, dramatic stories and powerful voices of opera, Carmen collected all the information she could about this music. She needed to gather every song possible, have them all ready to unravel into her Electus' mind.

This is so simple. She listened to a sad song from an opera called Madam Butterfly. Sometimes song searching was difficult work, but Carmen loved this music…how had she not discovered it till now? There was something just a little familiar about it, but nothing that Carmen could put her wingtip on.

Then the FLim changed to an opera about the Before country, Spain. And there on the stage was a fiery-eyed woman, her head thrown back as the music poured from her throat. Curls tumbled down her back in a riotous black waterfall; she commanded the spellbound attention of everyone seated before her. Carmen could feel every cell in her own body reacting, leaping and storming about in her system. It was heaven, this music.

Then there was a shift to another song. It was a little like the other – created by the same person, Carmen wondered? – but the singers were two men in fishermen's costumes, talking to each other in song. Carmen didn't know what they were saying, but she didn't need to. Their voices climbed high and dipped low, together and alone like two tigers - both roaring and shy - playing with and battling each other, all in the same breaths.

She was relaxed way back into the platform, completely lost in the music, when she realized what she was listening to.

The song from First Life! her mind shrieked. *The same song!* How had she not recognized it immediately? What kind of spell did this opera music have on her mind?

Without thinking, she ripped the green discs off her eyes and tugged the silver band from her head, from where it immediately withdrew into the air.

Her eyes weren't focused, and so it took a few seconds before she even saw Lev, sitting one platform over, or heard his slow clapping.

"Another crisis for the drama angel?" he mewled. Then he leaned in, conspiratorially. "Why don't you sell tickets? Ya know, you're never getting out of here on skill."

He looked over his shoulder…making sure God wasn't eavesdropping?

Then he hissed, "Maybe you can *buy* your way out."

Chapter 3

Carmen knew she wouldn't think of anything clever to say until five minutes after he'd disappeared, so she didn't bother trying.

Lev, brown-skinned and lanky, levelled his dark-browed eyes at her. "Don't you have an Electus, Princess Carmen? You know, a First Life who has to depend on *you* to find the song that will lead her peacefully from Before to the Sweet Hereafter?" There was a dramatic pause. Everything about Lev was dramatic. "Poor old thing."

"Is that how it works, Lev?" She paused, furrowing her brow as if deep in thought. "Hey, I get it...song angel. Song...angel!"

Carmen knew it wasn't much of a comeback, and Lev ignored it. "Otherwise, Princess, she'll end up here, like the rest of the losers, trying to solve the puzzle from First Life that'll get her to the Sweet Hereafter."

"Like you, Lev?" Did he wince, or did she just imagine it?

Lev started up again. "So don't you think maybe it would be a good idea for you to concentrate on finding that song, before your Electus croaks without it? She just might not wait for all your personal dramas to be wrapped up."

"Shove off! I don't have dramas. Well, hardly any..."

"Click! Click!" Lev held up an imaginary camera. "Here's Carmen, working with a bedridden man who listened to the same music every day...but you couldn't find that tune, could you? Wasn't there some kind of difficulty with you not using MindSupply for fear of getting information you didn't want about your own First Life?"

"That's not fair! He was my first, and how was I supposed to know that he loved that music? It was piped through the speakers all over the seniors' home, and he never once reacted to it. He seemed oblivious."

Lev just smirked.

"Even Zeke said that!"

"What about the dog, then?"

Carmen had to admit that the dog had been a surprise. Who knew that part of a song angel's work could be finding the right final song for an animal?

"I found the dog's! You know that!"

"The same way some First Life's parents *help* with their homework! Zeke did it all. You know that, Princess." He tossed his head away from her scornfully, his long, shaggy hair flipping from one side to the other.

Too much, too much. Carmen's head was bursting. What he was saying was wrong, yet as usual with Lev, Carmen couldn't find the words to make him understand. He poked and prodded at her until she bit back.

"We all know *you're* the perfect song angel, Lev." Carmen paused, loading herself like a gun with the bullet she was angry enough to deliver. "You never make a mistake." Another pause. "But we also know that you're still here, and your brother is in the Sweet Hereafter, isn't he?"

Carmen ignored the look she saw forming on Lev's face. "And just when are *you* going there, Lev?"

She knew he wouldn't strike her – it was too crucial to him to maintain his perfect angel reputation – but the look he flashed her before ripping his wings open and leaving her in a swirl of poisoned air was enough.

Dulcie's face was all attention this time when she appeared at Carmen's elbow. "What was that all about, Carmen?"

Carmen just stared at her for a moment, her brain dripping anger at Lev for continually misunderstanding everything she did, and guilt for having used his pain to get revenge. Slowly her mind settled onto Dulcie.

"Same old, Dulcie. For some reason, Lev hates me...but thanks for asking," Carmen responded. It was pretty amazing that Dulcie had managed to pull herself away from the lure of MindSupply. "I really appreciate it."

"No worries, and it's not just you Lev hates. It's the whole world, whichever world he happens to be in," Dulcie continued. She ran fingertips through the white-blonde wisps of hair that framed her fragile features. Carmen often thought that Dulcie exactly resembled how First Lives pictured angels: delicate and graceful, with a cloud of pale hair that just cried out for a halo. Carmen had never actually seen a halo. Did they even exist? Maybe angels in the Sweet Hereafter had them; maybe a halo was like a major bling reward for having sorted out all the messy issues of First Life. Who knew?

"Yeah, I guess. It always feels so personal when he's on the attack," Carmen said. "Why can't he just be the perfect, prissy, obsessive song angel he is, and leave out the nastiness? That can't be helping to get him to Sweet, can it?"

"Nope,'"was Dulcie's answer. "But I don't think he can control it. He does everything else perfectly, but he isn't perfect, or he wouldn't be here."

Lev, opera, Dulcie...Carmen was just too weary to feel anymore. "I need to rest, Dulcie. Can we talk later?" Dulcie was already looking back longingly at the

MindSupply platform she'd vacated. Carmen knew where she'd be in one minute.

Carmen propelled herself off MindSupply and into the ether, waiting for a hammock to appear. The glowing green bud was suddenly there, beginning slowly to unfurl as Carmen watched. She could hardly wait for it to blossom into the pillowy embrace that would cradle her into rest.

Once in, she settled her wings about her, let her eyes close, and was gone.

***

Where was Mezzo? Where was Before, for that matter? Carmen only knew that when she was in Mezzo and was heading for Before, she flew downward, then back up to return home. But Mezzo wasn't Heaven, she knew that. For one thing, it took only a few moments to reach one place from the other; no flying through the clouds and then the this-o-sphere and the that-o-sphere.

No puffy gold and pink clouds, and not a single harp, Carmen mused as she started the downward journey to her Electus. Then as an afterthought, *but Mezzo's just a stopover. Maybe Sweet is rolling with halos and pearly gates!* Somehow she doubted it, though. To dream up Heaven, somebody at sometime on Before must have had a pretty good imagination.

And so back to the original problem: where was Mezzo? It seemed to Carmen that it was all in some way joined – Before, Mezzo, the Sweet Hereafter, and who knew what else? – but at the same time separated by the thinnest yet strongest of curtains.

Then came another thought: was it okay to be sorting through all of this divine organization in her head, or was she just supposed to be taking the information given to her and accepting it? Would Zeke appreciate her thinking for herself?

Would God?

The sight of Marion's cottage blew all these thoughts aside. It was colder today, the kind of spring day not elegized by poets; the kind where daffodils huddled together for warmth, their yellow mouths open in a frozen expression of surprise.

Her Electus was inside. Inside wasn't entirely comfortable yet for Carmen – maybe she wasn't long enough away from this world not to feel trapped when back inside one of its buildings. And she didn't enjoy that little stomach lurch that came with passing through solid Before materials, but she knew her squeamishness was a luxury she couldn't afford.

You're never gonna be a great song angel – ha! even an adequate one, according to Lev – if you don't get past all that. Then she forced herself to the outside wall of the house, took a hiccupy breath in, and floated forward.

There was just that moment where it seemed her stomach might exit out through her eyes, then a settling, and she was inside. Was it getting easier? Maybe.

The cottage was small, so it was never hard to find her Electus. There were a few rooms on the main floor, and Carmen knew immediately that Marion was nowhere there. From upstairs, she could hear music again...opera?

Drat! It's some other kind of music. The more kinds of music an Electus liked, the harder it was to find their final piece, and she knew Marion's time was severely limited.

Although she knew herself to be invisible to First Lifes, she still felt more comfortable doing what she needed to do around them quickly, then disappearing. She'd spent very little time just looking around Before, because usually there was a First Life there, talking or humming or gazing off into space... watching her? No! But still, it was eerie.

So this time, feeling relaxed, Carmen did one float of the rooms downstairs. One whole room for eating! Fridge, to keep things cold, and oven, to warm them up (could they make up their minds?). In the next room, a piano in one corner, its wood polished to a gleam. If she closed her eyes and focused hard, Carmen's music antennae could sense the afternotes from the instrument tumbling in the air. Her Electus still played this piano.

I need to come back when she plays. Maybe that's where her final piece is?

She could hear the music from the room above, Marion's bedroom, so Carmen began the slow flutter up the stairs. Halfway up, a glint of light caught at a painting hung just above Carmen's eyes, and she lifted her head without thinking, to look at it.

On the canvas, a cloud of palest hair encircled a face too sweet for First Life. Wings spread wide, eyes searching upward toward a hand that was extended from above.

"Dulcie!" Carmen gasped. For it was she.

Chapter 4

Not.

Impossible! She eyed the picture carefully. *Marion did not whip out her cell phone at church and take this shot of God lending Dulcie a helping hand.* Carmen squinted even closer, then shook her head, realizing with some relief that it was a painting, not a photo.

I'd hate to find pictures like this, ones that looked so much like me that my friends could hardly tell the difference. What must it be like, to be the perfect angel prototype, like Dulcie?

As she continued upward, she gave an indelicate little angel snort. How many spiky black-haired angels showed up on the ceilings of chapels? Were pug noses streaming with freckles common in elegant churches? What about flashing green eyes? Carmen couldn't recall even one. A song angel she was, but typical...nope. She was on the pudgy side, like the angels of Renaissance painters, with dimply elbows and baby feet, but there the angelic resemblances stopped. Dulcie had her beat, hands down.

In the doorway of the bedroom, Carmen paused for a moment, her wings fanning slowly in the air. She watched her Electus, who again had the quilt spread over her legs, but this time in the bed. It was morning, but she looked tired already; she had probably been too weary after breakfast to do anything but fetch her quilt materials and head back to bed. Of course, she had had enough energy to organize the music that was playing, that was always playing. Marion's priority.

Still in the doorway, Carmen watched the old woman work. The needle slowly, painstakingly wove in and out, the tired hand coming down to rest often on the fabric. She had been working on the quilt for months, since before Carmen had been assigned to her. Carmen had wondered at first if she would complete it before her transition, but she could see now that it was almost done.

"I need to find that music!" a voice whispered urgently in her mind. This time it wasn't Zeke's voice, but a little part of her own brain urging her forward. Yet she lingered a moment more, just watching her Electus.

Every song angel felt a kind of benevolent affection mixed with professional obligation for their Electi. It was the way the whole system worked. And Carmen had felt that for each of hers, even that troublesome little dog. But as she watched, something different crept in now. Something more personal. More...human?

Marion suddenly looked up, startled by a sound. A bird call outside? She looked straight into Carmen's eyes. Just for a moment, suspended in the air, Carmen felt herself transported somewhere else, looking deep into a different pair of watery blue eyes, holding hers with a love and joy that she could feel down to her angel tippy-toes.

And then Carmen slid back into memories again, into that dark hallway. There was no warning and no means of escape. The door nearest her swung wide before she had even one moment to turn away. Inside the door sat a woman with gray-flecked hair and enormous purple-framed glasses. She was younger than Marion, but reminded Carmen of her, for some reason. She was seated at a table spread with a swirl of fabrics and thread. In her hands she held the edges of a quilt, only partially done. On her lap she held a small girl with black hair that hadn't listened to a comb; her pug nose was a freckle explosion. The woman was looking right into that small girl's eyes, holding them fast.

"And so," she was saying to the girl, "when you choose the fabric carefully, the quilt becomes a life's story, like a storybook of all the important things that happened to that person." The girl was listening intently, sitting still, which seemed to be something unusual for her. She picked up a piece of cloth and held it beside another, then exchanged it for one that seemed to suit her better. Carmen was only a flutter of wings; her whole essence was poured into the pair at the table.

"Kinda like my baby book," said the girl, "where I start out red and wrinkly, and now I'm just like me, and all the important things in between. Right, Granny?"

"Yes, that's it, dear. That's exactly it," the woman responded, and it was easy to see how pleased she was that the little one understood so well. Almost without thinking, Carmen reached for the lifechain that hung around her neck. It also told the story of a life, but that story was a hidden one.

There was a very large needle near some thick yarn on the table by the girl. Now the woman helped her thread it, and guided the girl's hand as she sewed the pieces of cloth she'd chosen. Eventually the grandmother resumed work on the large quilt, angling awkwardly around the child's body on her lap. There was a smaller chair nearby, but she made no move to transfer the child there.

Music was playing, and Carmen knew what it was now. Opera. A voice swirled around the room. After a while, the child extricated herself from her grandmother's lap and went to the middle of the room to swirl and dip with it. She threw back her head and with eyes closed, swayed to the notes like a feather on the wind. Her grandmother stopped to watch, then closed her eyes and got lost in the music, herself.

"What kind of song is this, Granny?"

The eyes behind the purple rims opened slowly. "It's called an aria," the woman explained. "The singer is a clown, and his song is about laughing on the outside while you feel sad inside."

"Oh, Granny. The poor clown."

The woman held out her arms, and the girl snuggled in.

Just then, a new sound came to Carmen's ears. As it did, the quilt, the woman and the girl faded, and with them, their music. And now a man's voice, smooth yet peppy, was seeking her ear, insisting on being heard. The door in her memory had closed, the hallway disappeared...and there her Electus lay again, back against her pillows, a small smile on her face. The needle had been carefully inserted into the quilt, and the fingers, instead of stitching, were now snapping.

"Frankie!" Marion murmured. "Ah...Frankie!" She swayed against her pillows; Carmen could see her feet dancing under the blankets. For a moment she wasn't an old woman in her bed, she was...well, Carmen didn't know where she was, but she wasn't here. From the expression on her face and what little Carmen had seen in FLims about Frank Sinatra's time, she was back 60 years, hair in a perky ponytail, socks rolled down under a wide skirt emblazoned with a poodle.

"You know you're old when the crazywild songs you danced to with your sweetheart end up pureed and poured like baby pablum through the loudspeakers in a store." There was a giggle in Marion's voice as she said it, and it made Carmen so glad. Finding the right song for dying Electi didn't usually have much to do with glad.

But it was time to test the music she'd researched. So Carmen pulled up the opera and carefully played each aria, each overture, each chorus. Carmen had learned a lot about opera. She pulled all the songs she'd collected, one at a time, through her Electus' brain channels.

She sat up when she heard that piece, Carmen noted. But it wasn't enough to know for sure. *She smiled at the ceiling when she heard that one!* Or did she? Carmen reeled each song out carefully, like a fisherman casting his nets over the waters, anxious to feel the nets heavy with fish. She came up with zero.

Carmen glanced again at the quilt. Almost done, almost time. How many songs would it take before she heard the right one? She was frustrated, but almost glad for the static that the frustration produced in her brain, blocking out the scene she'd witnessed between the grandmother and girl in the hall. And their words, still echoing in her brain.

The only good thing about all that is at least I know why I'm feeling different about Marion. I'm not supposed to care that way. This is a job, and it's too important to get muddled up with feelings. It obviously has something to do with what I saw behind that door. Then another thought came. *Man, what would Zeke say? More lectures, probably. But at least now I know it has something to do with that little kid and her grandmother...* She left the thought to trail away, not wanting to admit, even to herself, that she knew who the two were.

She let her Electus, the ticking clock and the powerful music fill her mind. She wanted that other door slammed completely shut, and in her mind, she did just that.

"Work to do! No time for all that!"

She left her Electus bent over her quilt, Frankie's crooning restored. The trip back to Mezzo was longer, harder, and grumpier than the trip down had been.

***

Song angel work was exhausting. Becoming familiar with your Electus, searching for the clues in their life that led to finding the correct final piece. Then the energy it took to pipe the songs through their brain channels. And after all that, you were... wrong. Like now. Carmen knew it meant more trips to MindSupply, gathering more melodies to present to her Electus.

And will I do it in time? What if she goes into transition before I can find it? The pressure was mind-numbing, too.

The Fountain! The thought came in a rush, and Carmen knew it was the right one. *I know what I need to do, and I want to do it before Zeke suggests it.* She felt as though ChannelZeke was zoning in on her, and that was the last thing she needed now.

She moved through the shine and green-to-blue of Mezzo, feeling her way to the Fountain. Tendrils of multicolored gauze spiraled past Carmen, gently floating around anything that came near them. It had taken Carmen a while to figure out that the tendrils were sensors that controlled the scents of Mezzo. She'd flown near one in her early days there and was struck by the scent of baby powder, which she hated. In a millisecond, however, the powder smell was replaced by a faint lilac scent. Carmen found herself hovering near the tendril, breathing deeply and feeling calm. How did it know that baby powder made her headachy? How did it know that lilacs soothed her? Another Mezzo mystery.

As Carmen winged her way to the Fountain, others flew sedately past her. Higher, lower, nodding gently as they passed. She knew many here, but often there wasn't a reason to speak.

When the Fountain appeared, she eased in front of it, waiting for the energy flow to begin. She felt it first on all the front surfaces of her body, like the first touch of warm sun after a cold winter. Gradually it eased its way throughout her system like a massage, like the smell of fresh cut oranges, like everything that was renewing and energizing.

It was a good thing First Lifes didn't know anything about the Fountain, Carmen thought for the hundredth time, or that whole chew-and-swallow process of eating for fuel would seem pretty lame. She watched the Fountain, fascinated as always by the way the...flame? fluid?...rose up through the air, but also cascaded downwards simultaneously – up and down, all at once. Just watching it soothed Carmen, and pumped her full of energy.

Are they droplets, or flamelets? She leaned in to the Fountain and peered at it. She was still squinting when she felt someone settle beside her, and turned to find Zeke there. He had a real talent for catching her at very un-song-angel-like behavior.

"Or maybe I'm at it so often that it's hard for him to miss," she muttered. "Hi there, Zeke. What brings you here?"

What followed was a little Zekefommercial about angelic behavior...I know you're relatively new, but these wing-chasing and Lev-baiting incidents (*ooo, he'd actually heard that!*) are somewhat frequent...about finding her Electus' music quickly..."She is coming dangerously close to transition, and she is a candidate for the Sweet Hereafter" (thanks, Zeke; no pressure there)…and if her shoulders weren't already so droopy that her wingtips brushed her toes, about working with her own First Life…"Mature acceptance of the information offered you and how you deal with it are crucial to your existence here in Mezzo, and to your eventual successful passage into the Sweet Hereafter."

"Lord," Carmen muttered out loud. She wasn't sure if she was talking to someone in particular, or just plain overwhelmed.

"You're doing so many things so well," Zeke's silky voice continued. "Don't be discouraged, Carmen." Geez, he must have been a teacher in First Life. Carmen wondered if the scolding or the positive reinforcement was more painful.

With a beatific smile, he floated away – didn't he ever flap? Lurch? Wobble?

"I doubt it," Carmen groused.

And just to make a perfect moment even more perfect, Lev landed beside her. At least she didn't have to worry about the positive reinforcement part anymore.

"Oh look! Everyone's favorite remedial song angel." And then, "If your pal Dulcie was here, I'd think it was half price day for losers at the Fountain."

"Not up to your usual standards, Lev," Carmen responded, still staring straight into the Fountain. "You're slipping."

"Since when does your opinion count?" And then Lev leaned toward Carmen, brought his chocolaty eyes level with hers and hissed, "No more about my brother, ok? It isn't up for discussion." Carmen tilted nervously away from him, in spite of the fact that she was desperately searching for an evil comeback. "You keep it up, and I'll arrange it so you never get out of here. Not ever." He was watching her face intently, reading her expression. "Don't think I can? Try me."

Okay, it was all she had. A threat for a threat. "You want me to lay off, then you'd better leave both of us – Dulcie and me – alone. I know all about your brother, Lev. Thaddeus, isn't it? I know why you're here, and why he's in the Sweet Hereafter." She didn't, of course; the brother's name was just something she'd once overhead Lev mumbling. But bullies in Mezzo were no better than those in First Life, and Carmen couldn't think of any other way to get Lev off her back. If he thought she knew his story, would he stop?

His eyes bled venom now. "Don't you even say his name, or I'll..." He stared at her until she felt the tiny feathers on her wings tremble. Then he soared off in another Lev tornado. Did he ever just say "See you later!" and fly away?

And how did he get away with this bully stuff? Did he not have a commander? Carmen was surprised that Zeke wasn't rearing up in front of her with tips for interangel relations. He must figure she needed to work this one out alone.

Which, in a way, I hate.Mostly I'd just like to wring Lev's neck. But even though I don't know what it is, there's obviously something so painful about his brother that it kind of creeps me out to keep needling him about it. This is one thing I could actually use Zeke's help with, and for some reason ChannelZeke is on a station break.

Even after dealing with Zeke and Lev, Carmen still felt at least somewhat better than she had when she first arrived back in Mezzo – that Fountain was truly amazing! – so she decided to find Dulcie.

Do angels do girlfriend time? Whatever. It's probably called angel interlocution or something, but it's girlfriend time for me.

***

Carmen found Dulcie in a hover, eyes gazing off while her fingers picked absentmindedly at the feathers on her wings.

"What are you doing, Dulcie?!?" Carmen chided, her eyes on the fingers pulling at the already-patchy feathers. "You're going to be the first bald-winged song angel in Mezzo history, if you keep that up."

Dulcie's eyes suddenly snapped into focus and her mouth twisted down into a pout, ready to defend or deny. Then there was a moment where the two angels just looked at each other, while the image of a bald-winged Dulcie floating through Mezzo settled on them.

Dulcie was the first to laugh, Carmen a close second. They doubled over, clutching at their stomachs while their wings tippled forward, partially opened, unsure.

Dulcie gasped, "Yeah, and you'll be the rotisserie angel, when Lev finally figures out how to exact his revenge on you…"

So funny! They laughed and shrieked together. It was almost as relaxing as the Fountain, Carmen thought, as she wiped laugh dribbles from her eyes.

Snap! Both were suddenly upright, laughter gone, smoothing their rumpled robes. They looked at each other, eyebrows lifted.

"Did you get a message, just now?" Dulcie asked. "From your commander?"

"Yup," came the answer. "You?"

"Yup again. Clear, quiet as a mouse, brutally gentle...STOP."

Amazing, always amazing around here. How did two different angel commanders work that at once? Were they linked? One creature with two bodies?

"Wow," they both breathed. Which almost started them off again. Luckily, another favorite topic led them away from that discussion.

Fashion. "I still can't believe this fabric," Carmen muttered, fingering her robe. "Wrinkles like crazy, everything sticks to it..." Here she pulled at a white-blonde strand on Dulcie's shoulder. "I sure hope that when we finally get to the Sweet Hereafter, we won't be dealing with clothing issues for all eternity. It's just nasty."

"You know what I'd like? A couple more outfits. Some more mix-and-match pieces would be good," Dulcie responded. "Do they really expect us to wear the same robe all the time?"

"The only good thing about these robes is the temperature," Carmen went on, feeling massively relieved that they were safely out of laughing territory. She'd had enough of Zeke lecturing her for one day. Not that laughing was forbidden or anything, but Carmen was pretty sure Zeke wouldn't think this was such a productive use of her time.

"Temperature?"

"Yeah. You know how you always stay cool when it's hot, and warm when it's cold?"

"Carmen?" Dulcie was starting to laugh again, much to Carmen's horror. She was trying to hold it in, but her tiny frame was starting to shake, her blonde curls were tremoring hopelessly.

"It's not the fabric," she wheezed, barely able to speak. And of course, now Carmen had started up again, feeling the bubbles of laughter rise out of her throat and pop open in her brain and mouth.

"Oh yeah, I forgot..." Angels *did* have stomach muscles, because hers were now killing her. "It's because...

Dulcie hooted now, screaming with laughter. "It's because..."

They chorused together, "We're DEAD!!"

Chapter 5

Laughing like hyenas, they almost didn't hear the faint sound of the bells at first. It began in a tremor, as if the slightest breeze had rippled past a patch of bluebells. It grew wider and wilder in moments, so they heard it just as the first winds blew by them, whipping their robes and hair frantically. It was impossible to keep laughing. As was required, they unfurled their wings and pushed with their powerful muscles toward the Fountain.

It was hard work. The bells were now clanging so loudly that it felt as if they flew against not only the wind, but against the bells themselves. And the air was filled with song angels, all moving in the same direction. The rhythmic back and forth glide of countless wings added to the maelstrom of wind and sound; the clanging intensified until it seemed to originate inside Carmen's head. The bells pulled the angels forward, like marionettes on strings.

As they neared the Fountain, they could see only its top half, rising above the throng of angels gathered for the ceremony. Its usual gentle prism of rainbow colors was intensified into vivid slashes of fuschia and emerald, each color blazing and fading as new ones emerged; it boiled up and tumbled down like lava, its power barely contained.

Carmen and Dulcie folded their wings, easing into stillness, and waited. Their wait was not long. Slowly, a figure appeared in the Fountain, rising from amongst the angel throng to where he was visible to the pair. He was already an angel, but naked, wings and body curled up in a ball like a fetus, like a tiny gerbil. His hands shielded his head as if to say "Enough! I have had enough! No more. Please." Small wonder; he had just died on Before, and now found himself in a completely foreign place. His face was worn and creased; he looked so old and so new. Carmen found it hard to watch, but she did, because she knew what came next.

New song angels were a relatively rare occurrence in Mezzo. Doubtless in the Sweet Hereafter, arrivals were commonplace – Carmen imagined a turnstile, never stopping, or a rotating glass door, with a constant flood of newbies floating in. But most First Lifes did not become song angels. Most had their final song playing in their brains as they died, allowing them to move straight from Before to the Sweet Hereafter. Only those whose music remained a mystery were reborn in Mezzo, as was happening with this new song angel.

Carmen liked the ceremony. She watched as the figure slowly uncurled and looked around, his head staying motionless while his eyes darted from one sight to another. For just a moment he seemed panic-struck, and then his face relaxed into calm, his body began to open. And from his shoulders, his wings gently unfurled. As they watched, he rotated slowly above them, while his wings, as bare and pink as he, stretched out and up. Then a robe was eased over his head and wings. The fabric might be terrible, but at least they came with slits for wings.

Carmen felt her eyes wandering to the throng of song angels surrounding the Fountain. As a unit, they flowed in and ebbed out from the Fountain's volcanic colors, as if giant angel contractions were helping this new one to form.

And now the part Carmen found the most interesting. She looked above his head expectantly, and saw the chain begin to form. She saw bits and pieces of she-knew-not-what fly from every direction in a blaze of light and color and sound, like iron particles to a magnet, until the chain was whole and ready to be lowered. She watched it descend around his head and rest over his collarbone. It fit there like a glove, the chain around his neck, the pendant hanging down his back.

Carmen looked down at her own. She could barely feel its weight, but it was strong, stronger than any metal on Before, and she knew the chain and pendant were totally unbreakable. She glanced at Dulcie, whose back was to her, and looked at the pendant that hung off the chain between her wings. As with all song angels, it was formless, a silvery cloud waiting to be shaped, and then discarded. Only when a song angel was ready to ascend to the Sweet Hereafter would the pendant form into any discernible shape. For Dulcie, who'd been so long in Mezzo, it had been a long wait.

Carmen floated forward to her friend. "Dulce," she began in a whisper, "do you remember your transition?"

"Yes," was the answer. "Do you?"

"Yup." A pause. "I wish I'd looked up to see my lifechain forming." She kept her voice low, as the ceremony wasn't quite over. Soon the new song angel's commander would appear, and take him off to begin his work in Mezzo.

"You know how it goes, Carmen. Everything that happened to you in First Life – every stranger's smile, that spelling test you blew in Grade 2, your first kiss…did you have a first kiss? I didn't have time… melds together to make your chain."

"I know, I know," Carmen said. As if reading from a textbook, she droned, "All experiences are forged into the lifechain, all knowledge and experience from First

Life, which will be carried into Mezzo and eventually, into the Sweet Hereafter."

"Wow! That's good," Dulcie said.

"But the pendant, that's what gets me," Carmen continued. "Look at mine again, ok? It's really just a blob, right?"

"Carmen, I've looked at yours a million times. You know they're all blobs. They represent why we're here, and they won't become any particular something until we figure it out, sort it out, and move on to Sweet."

"It just seems weird, that they're so mysterious," responded Carmen. "Wouldn't you like to know what it is, to help you figure out why you're here?"

"I know why I'm here," Dulcie said quietly.

The ceremony was now over. Song angels moved away, singly or in small groups. There was a ruffled feeling in the air, as if the arrival of the First Life, the new song angel, had reminded the others of where they'd left, where they were going...and why they weren't there yet.

Carmen jolted around to face Dulcie. "You know? Why? And..." She had been about to say - why are your wings still so bare, if you know more about your life than I do about mine? – but changed her mind. Even angel buddies had limits.

Dulcie didn't answer at first, and Carmen didn't think she was going to at all. But then came, "I left Before because I was hit by a car. I was walking home from school with my little sister, and the car was suddenly..." She stopped, staring at Carmen, but not seeing her at all.

"You didn't hear your music? Nothing?"

"It was too fast, I guess. All I could hear was my sister, screaming and screaming." Dulcie's voice was getting hard to hear, fading to a childlike whisper.

"Most First Lifes *do* hear their music at the end, even if their transition is fast," Carmen went on, watching Dulcie's face carefully.

But she'd made a mistake, gone too far. Dulcie smiled a tiny smile, shook her head and abruptly arched her body away from Carmen. Her wings opened and she was gone.

Carmen held her hands up to Dulcie, her fingers reaching, as she flew away. It almost felt as if her fingers could knead through the air Dulcie had left behind, feel the bumpy pain of it.

But that was impossible. Dulcie had disappeared, and Carmen knew where she was headed. Toward MindSupply, toward forgetfulness.

Chapter 6

Chocolate. Chocolate. Carmen rolled the word around in her head, wondering at the buzzy feeling in her mind and stomach when she thought about it. She loved the Fountain, loved its instant energy. Imagine all that chewing work, just to get some fuel! But somehow, chocolate seemed different.

She watched Marion put another piece in her mouth. She was moving slowly about the kitchen, washing her teacup, drying it off, putting it in the cupboard, but her face was all about the chocolate. Hands working, mouth and mind melting with that little brown square of magic.

Suddenly, Carmen wanted some. Just one little square. It was just chocolate…what could it hurt? She quickly checked ChannelZeke. No one there.

She floated toward the open package on the table, glad to see that a small piece was broken off. Like moving through walls on Before, lifting objects wasn't yet effortless for Carmen, but with a little concentration, she could manage it. She wasn't sure she could have broken the piece off, though.

Okay, hoist it up...think UP...yeah, that's it. Now right inside your mouth and… She closed her eyes, waiting for the creamy melt to begin. Instead, the square of chocolate dropped through her like a skydiver without a parachute. She stared blankly down at the floor, where it had bounced under the table.

If you can float through walls, I guess having a Before mouth and stomach to hold chocolate just isn't an option. The best she could do was to watch her Electus look around the room, perplexed, and then slowly reach down to retrieve the coveted piece. She dusted it off and placed it on her tongue. Then she collected her quilt bag, the quilt itself and headed outside to her chair under the still-blossoming tree.

This time there was no music. Carmen hoped she hadn't spooked Marion in the house - where chocolate rolled magically onto the floor - before she could organize her music. But then she sensed something different.

The quilt was almost finished, with only two squares left to be sewn in. Her Electus sighed, her head nodded for a moment, and then she bent forward and jabbed the needle into the fabric. There was no time for music now. This quilt must be finished…today, now. The time was so near.

And so Carmen floated gently, close to her Electus, to her old ears, and began to hum every song she had collected. She started with all the opera she knew, and then every Frank Sinatra song she had filed away. The angel hum that emanated from Carmen came into the old woman's ears as full-blown music, complete with orchestra and back-up singers. But there was no click, no look of recognition or understanding on Marion's face. There was no sign that she could hear the music at all; her face reflected only the fierce concentration of one with a little too much work left to do in the time allotted.

The sharp jangle of the phone from the cottage got the same response…nothing. It kept ringing, ringing, ringing. The old woman's eyes darted left briefly, but then came back to her quilting.

Have to find the song. She only has one foot left on Before. Soon she'll have left there altogether. She continued the hum, watching Marion's eyes for even a flicker of interest or recognition. Again, nothing. The quilt, at this point, was the only existence she had left on Before.

Carmen felt panic rising inside her; she'd been here before, and knew that no matter how short the time, the panic would only prevent her from completing her assignment. In an effort to relax, she let go of the humming and looked down at the quilt.

The final piece of quilt, now being painstakingly worked in by the old woman's wobbly fingers, was white fabric strewn with pastel baby handprints. Looking at it, Carmen felt an immediate sense of anxiety. *Great.* Her stomach and brain were texting panic messages back and forth. *Take one cup of panic, add two tablespoons of stomach flip flops, stir well and...* But that was as far as she got. Next thing she knew, she was inside that dark hallway again. She was not ready to face more memories, but she had no choice. The door nearest to her was open, and she could hear the smallest cry, just a whimper really, coming from a cradle in the corner. A baby lay there, legs kicking, eyes looking into the opposite corner at something...or someone.

So sweet. And yet, some other uncomfortable feeling was worming its way into her, maggot-like.

Carmen eased herself a little further into the doorway, looking to where the baby's eyes searched.

A girl stood there. She clutched a baby quilt, white with pastel handprints. She hoisted it up in the air as if it were a trophy. The girl had spiky black hair and a strip of freckles across her nose; on her face was a look of satisfaction mixed with shame. She looked to be about eight years old. Carmen knew immediately who that little girl was.

And then a voice came from outside, down the dark hallway. "Carmen, the baby is starting to cry. Maybe he's kicked off his blanket. Could you make sure he's tucked in?"

Listening, Carmen could feel every part of her body stiffen. Even her wings tightened into a feathery knot. She knew that voice, that baby, and of course, that girl in the corner. She didn't at that moment like the girl much, and she definitely didn't like how she was feeling about the baby. What could a baby have done to make her feel this way?

She watched the girl cross the room, drop the blanket in a single motion over the baby and then walk straight toward Carmen. It was only at that moment that Carmen heard music. It was that particular music, the men's voices again cresting together, the two fishermen from the MindSupply FLim, and from her first visit to this hall of memory, or whatever it was. The opera was playing loudly down the hall. She saw the girl's face register the music and gain a kind of peace from that, and watched her take one scornful look back at the baby. Then she swooshed through Carmen before Carmen had a chance to move, leaving her feeling sliced open. The room faded, the baby was gone… and it was just Carmen again, floating over her Electus.

The music's end drifted through her body, and so she hummed it softly, without thinking. She hovered in the air, wings spread, feeling a kind of calm now. Marion's eyes closed, opened, and she pulled the last golden stitch through. Only the final knot to tie now.

Carmen hummed a little louder, and suddenly, the old woman's eyes flared wide, and she let the needle drop. There was a smile, and then her head dropped off to one side. She was perfectly still.

It was over. Marion was free.

I didn't try that one song, all this time, because of those memories. She watched her now-still Electus, so peaceful. *The fishermen's song, that duet. I heard it in MindSupply, and I heard it twice in that hallway in my memory.* That hall *was* her memory; Carmen knew that now. *But I couldn't use that song because I was too freaked out hearing it.* For a being of the air, Carmen felt as heavy as lead. *Marion could have been safe, so long ago, if only I had.* She felt a tremor of ChannelZeke, tuned in but silent. Ah, the best teacher, happy to stay still if she learned the lesson the most powerful way, all by herself.

Carmen knew there were only moments left before her Electus began the climb upward to the Sweet Hereafter, and she needed to be gone. But she flew in close, and used her fingers – almost as wobbly as Marion's had been – to tie that final knot, to finish off the quilt and the old woman's story on Before.

As she did so, she heard the phone begin its jingle jangle again. This time, after all the rings had ceased, a voice came on, leaving a message that Marion would never hear.

The voice was a man's, old and full of love.

"Sister, it's me. Robert. I'm wondering how you are, and wanting you to know that I'm thinking about you. And just to tell you...oh, it's silly, really...but I wanted you to know that you've been the best possible sister to me, all of our long lives. I love you. Goodbye, dear."

With a strange emptiness in her throat that had nothing to do with chocolate, Carmen fanned her wings and reached for the sky.

Chapter 7

"This angel work ethic is ridiculous," Carmen muttered to herself as she floated into MindSupply, searching out a vacant platform. "I just got back to Mezzo. I'm exhausted, and already I have another Electus to worry about?"

She settled back and made herself comfortable, waiting for the silver trail to find her head, circle it and present the infamous cucumbers to her eyes. Her head throbbed slightly and her wings felt heavy as granite, but a small part of her was feverish to find out about her next assignment. This work and all it involved – the excruciating pressure of helping an Electus end a life in peace, no matter how their transition came – was terrifying and exhausting; but for Carmen, it was also exhilarating and energizing. She loved it.

MindSupply, with its usual spooky knowing, gave Carmen lots of time with calming music and images first, smoothing the ruffled and tired spots in her mind and body to milky pudding. Then came a story, one she followed with interest, taking her mind completely away from her own concerns. Then even a little angel humor. There was no remote control for her, no choice involved. Just Carmen and the omniscient presence that was MindSupply, filling needs and gaps that she didn't even know she had.

So she was almost ready when the FLim began. It was the girl again, with the spiky black hair and freckles. Carmen wanted to keep those curtains, the ones slowly opening for her on the story of her own First Life, completely closed.

It ain't happenin'. Then she sighed and gave up. *I might as well pay attention, because I'm gonna have to watch it, whether I want to or not.* What happened to rebel angels? She didn't relish the thought of being hauled away in cucumber chains.

The girl was sitting between a man and a woman in an ornate theater. They leaned back into red velvet seats, a domed roof painted with gods and goddesses – and angels! – in golds and blues over their heads. The girl held each parent's hand, and all three were intently focused on the stage. There, a raven-haired women sang, arms thrown wide and head back.

Carmen watched the singer, so familiar, but mostly she watched the girl. She wore an elegant dress of green and purple velvet, with something gold shimmering through it. *I know that dress, that fabric.*

Carmen watched the child whisper to one parent – the tiny, bright-faced woman – and then the other – the dark-haired, freckly man. They smiled, squeezed her hand. She was planted so solidly and happily between them.

That little girl is the center of their world. Everything revolves around her.

In her mind for a moment came darkness, as the FLim switched to another scene. In that moment, Carmen came to a place where she could not call her "the girl" anymore, where that seemed too much like ostrich-in-the-sand behavior.

"That's me," she said. She even said it out loud. Then she said it again. "That's me." And once she'd said it, her wings felt a little lighter, her mind felt a little less gray, a little more sweet blue. It was a relief.

The new FLim came on.

Now they were in a café, seated in a room full of candles with a mishmash of posters and photographs on the walls. Seated on a stool, a violinist swayed slowly to his own silvery melodies.

The girl....*no, not "the girl". Me*...was seated at a table, again squarely between both parents. Carmen looked carefully at each parent, now that she was acknowledging who they were to her. Her eyes moved from one to the other, greeting, remembering, memorizing. Her mother's eyes were green, glowing now as she took Carmen's hand and began to speak.

"We've been waiting for the right moment to tell you, honey," with a soft look at her husband, whose smile was tinged with a nervous edge. He took over, speaking carefully.

"We, all of us, are so lucky. We're going to have…," here he stopped for a moment, "…a baby!"

Carmen's mother reached forward to hug Carmen. "Finally, you'll get a chance to be the wonderful big sister I know you'll be. And you'll have company! Someone to…" She murmured on, not seeing Carmen's face. Her father was silent and tilted away a little, watching Carmen.

I remember this. I know what's going to happen next. I don't have to keep watching. But she did. She watched as young Carmen leapt to her feet, and stared at both her parents in shock.

"I don't need company! We have each other. You have *me*!" Before either parent could move, she bolted for the door and wrenched it open. The look of happy expectation was wiped from her mother's face, and her father's gentle watchfulness shifted into a body tensed to leap, to protect Carmen from whatever she might do next. Outside it was dark and cold, but she ran forward into it...anywhere but that sweet, false scene behind her.

She wasn't enough! She wasn't enough. They needed another someone to make their lives complete. Someone who would take endless time and attention, cry whenever it felt like it, keep them at home burping and cuddling instead of going out with Carmen. Who needed a *baby?*

Carmen was back there now, feeling the panic almost as acutely as she had the first time. The angel's and the girl's minds were meshing; Carmen could hardly tell who or where she was.

The girl was running now, and the parents panicked, pushing open the door, running into the street. The FLim started to fade. Carmen's whole being throbbed with the memory of it.

She lay back against the MindSupply platform, caught somewhere between First Life and now, a small angel spinning slowly in nothingness. Her eyes closed. She allowed the blackness to overcome her; she knew the curtain would open again on her First Life, but for now, she shoveled the rest of recall away for later, and was grateful for this calm black.

***

From above, everything on Before looked simple. In cities, people walked their dogs and polished their cars; in the country, brooks meandered and groves of trees fluttered their leaves when the wind passed by. All the really complicated stuff seemed to happen inside heads and hearts, and happily for Carmen, you couldn't see that from above.

She just wanted to float and fly, to feel the cool air graze her forehead and lift her wings. She concentrated on the slow folding and swelling motions of her flight. She stayed high up, where the air currents tossed and flipped her, and where only the big picture on Before was evident.

But eventually, the pull of Before – glorious warts and all – was too much, and Carmen let herself settle to flying just over the street lights and buildings. She kept reminding herself that no First Life could see her.

She directed her eyes to work on navigation only, but as usual, they did what they wanted. Everywhere she looked, Carmen seemed to find a mother and son flying a kite, a brother and sister out for a walk, a girl helping her father carry groceries home.

Enough already. She ran her hand through the spikes of black that passed for her hair. *I wanted a rest, not a Perfect Families Tour.* Suddenly this flight didn't seem like such a hot idea, and for the first time in a while, Carmen felt a creeping awareness of being high in the air. She didn't like it, and could only glance down now and then for a peek at Before.

I'm an angel…how can I be scared of heights? she scolded herself. *I keep wanting to hold on to something…feel like I might fall forward…but I'm flying! I'm an angel! How could I fall forward?*

But the feeling wouldn't go away. Carmen adjusted her flight to prepare to enter Mezzo. She glanced down to Before one last time as she began her ascent.

Lev. There was Lev.

He was standing in a cemetery, just back from a large group of First Lives gathered around a hungry-looking hole in the ground. A coffin rested near the hole, ready to give back to Before the parts not needed after transition. Carmen could hear the sobs, she could feel grief swirling around amongst the gravestones like thick mud.

Sad, yes, but transition was her job now, and she understood its place on the longer journey. She knew that the First Life being buried below was long gone, probably well settled into the Sweet Hereafter.

She stayed up high, hoping Lev's concentration on what lay before him would prevent him from looking up and seeing her. Why was he still hanging around his Electus, when his job was so clearly over?

"This is so weird," Carmen murmured. "Against the rules, even." The rules were very clear; song angels were to play their Electus' final piece, stay with them as they passed, and then get out of the way as the transition began. She watched him carefully, saw him slide back against the gravestone behind him, and lean his head against it.

He's not watching the ceremony. Why is he even there? Then Carmen sensed another feeling tugging at her, something more than the swirl of grief from the funeral below. This one was an ache, a keening so strong that it cut through the other sadness like a siren. Carmen could almost see it pouring from Lev, and then she knew why he was here.

This wasn't about an Electus at all.

Carmen angled herself above Lev so her sightline would allow a glimpse of the gravestone he leaned on. She could see only one word, but it was the one she'd expected: Thaddeus.

Lev was actually haunting – did angels haunt? – his brother's grave. Also against the rules. After transition, a song angel's previous existence on Before was over.

Electus work was there, having a look around was okay…but hanging out at your brother's grave?

"I don't think so," Carmen said. She thought of all Lev's venom, of all the times he'd poured his nastiness onto her like a poisonous waterfall. And she felt like blowing a whistle, calling the angel commanders in to witness this imperfection in their star pupil.

Then she looked at his limp body, wings crushed and drooping against Thaddeus' stone. Just for a moment, her mind marveled at Lev's love for his brother.

What does that feel like? She thought back to her own First Life reaction to her sibling. Wasn't it normal to love your sibling like Lev did? Then what was the matter with her?

Below her, Lev raised his hands to his eyes. Did angels cry? She didn't want to get close enough to see.

She could still feel his agony, swirling up and away from him like a cloud of mosquitoes. Instinctively, she reached out with her hands to soothe him, let him know that someone else was there. Even though it was Lev. Even though.

And he looked up. Immediately. He dropped his hands and jerked his head up, instantly finding Carmen above him with his eyes, those pain-filled eyes.

Carmen didn't know what to do, so she just stared back at Lev, her hands still floating over his sadness until it just…disappeared.

Chapter 8

What disappears? Carmen tried to think back to her life on Before. Nothing disappeared, really. Flip flops or Math books might seem to disappear, but there they were eventually...under the couch or at the bottom of your locker, under a two week sediment of half-eaten lunches. First Lifes didn't just disappear, although it might feel that way to loved ones when one slipped away as unexpectedly as Carmen had; she still didn't know much about her own First Life, but she had some sense of her transition. Balancing, and then suddenly, no balance at all. Then she'd been gone from Before, but not disappeared. Not at all.

And feelings. On First Life, as in Mezzo, feelings didn't just disappear. They lessened, they swelled, they slid sideways into other feelings, but they did not disappear. And yet, as Carmen watched Lev, the harsh feelings that had been erupting from him seemed to do just that.

At first Lev stared up at her, his face mottled by that mixture of pain and hate she'd seen so many times before. But slowly, as she let her hands hover over the waves of air coming from him – charged air, so full of tears and bile that she could feel the molecules jumping against her skin – his face cleared. He continued to stare at her, still slumped against his brother's gravestone, but his wings began to lift and the eyes that gazed back at her were confused but venom-free for the first time that Carmen could ever remember.

As shovelful after sad shovelful of dirt was scooped onto the coffin in the hole, Carmen and Lev remained frozen, eyes locked.

I did that! The thought finally flitted into Carmen's bewildered brain. *I don't know how, but I took those feelings away from Lev.* Below, Lev was fluttering his wings, looking at the ground, at the First Lifes, at anything except Carmen. She looked down at her hands in amazement, remembering the impulse to soothe the air as it boiled up to her. *How did I know how to do that?* For a moment, she remembered combing the air behind Dulcie after she had suddenly flown away, upset. What was going on?

She watched as Lev chose a flight path far away from her for his re-entry into Mezzo. He didn't know how to deal with this either. But he did look better. Almost happy, at least for now.

Carmen hovered alone. *I don't know how, but somehow for now, those feelings have just... disappeared.*

Chapter 9

Zeke was waiting for her when she got back. She'd been expecting it; she had a hunch that the grand plan had been to assign her next Electus the last time she'd been at MindSupply, but her reaction to the FLim about her First Life had nixed that. By Mezzo standards, this new assigning was overdue.

Carmen felt like an overcharged battery, tingling and round-eyed, after her experience with Lev. As it had when she'd first arrived, Mezzo's musical background poured over her in waves, coasting through her tissues and playing up and down her spine like a piano. Her senses were going crazy; she could see sounds and hear smells even more than was usual in Mezzo. It left her completely…

"Exhausted! I'm whipped, Zeke," she told her commander. "I can't concentrate on anything right now." Zeke, full of infuriating, serene knowledge as always, nodded slowly. He asked her what she'd like to talk about instead. Why did Carmen always feel that he knew her answers before he asked the questions?

"This weird hands thing. Do you know about that?" She didn't even want to look his way, because she knew he would definitely know something.

"A little. But what do *you* know about it?"

Aaaggghhh! The self-discovery method again. She had a sudden vision of Zeke, his pointy little goatee jutting out over a clipboard, taking notes while she lay on a couch confessing thousands of hours worth of problems.

What a waste of time! Why doesn't he just tell me everything I need to know? That wasn't what she said, however. What was the point?

"I know that Lev was..." She stopped there. *Hmmm...just leave out the part about where she'd found him...why complicate things?* She tried again. "He was feeling horrible about something. About Thaddeus, as usual. All this wicked energy was pouring out of him, and I don't know why I did it, but I just reached out and started touching that energy with my hands."

"What happened then?"

As if you don't know. Carmen found her tired mind wandering. Zeke had the nicest goatee. And glasses! Why would there be vision problems in the afterlife? He also had excellent arm muscles, Carmen noted. Was there a weight room in the grooming chamber she'd never noticed?

"Carmen? What happened?"

Oops. Need to concentrate. "The feelings just... went away. Lev looked peaceful. He looked really confused, but believe me, there were two of us feeling like that. I'm pretty sure he was happy." Here she paused for emphasis. "Lev. Happy!" She stared meaningfully at Zeke, but there was no response.

"So? What's up with that?" she continued. "What's on the agenda for song angel education today?"

Zeke raised one eyebrow at her, probably wondering at his questionable luck in being assigned this cranky song angel.

"You have a gift, Carmen. You've basically figured it out for yourself today. I'm surprised it took you this long, actually."

Thank you sir. "Why do I have this gift?" Carmen had been in Mezzo long enough to know that there was a purpose to everything.

"I don't know why you've got it."

Had she heard correctly? Zeke didn't know something?

"It's up to you to use it as you see fit. It could be a huge help...or a hindrance."

Great. More responsibility, more stuff to think about...could she not just sit back, paint her toenails and listen to some very loud music?

"One thing I do know is that you and your hands have the ability to find positive, uplifting feelings in other beings that they may not have tapped into themselves. What you are doing is ferreting this out, then somehow reflecting it back at them hugely magnified."

So she was a honking big piece of aluminum foil, reflecting goodness back like a giant tanning machine.

"A little warning, Carmen." His always-serious face looked even more so now. "Your abilities are for song angels only. That much I do know. Your hands are meant to help song angels struggling in Mezzo." He stopped meaningfully here. "And that is it." Very quiet now. "Never use it on Before. Never."

Well, duuh...that would be changing First Life history. Doesn't he think I know anything?

"Any more questions?" Zeke continued, obviously anxious to move on to her next Electus. "Ask away. This is important, Carmen." The only questions Carmen could think of were: 'Do you know where the receipt is for this gift?' and 'Would it be possible to return it?' She didn't think it would work too well to ask those. So she just smiled meekly and shook her head. Again she was wondrously glad for the fact that he could only broadcast inside her head, not hear her thoughts.

Anxious though he seemed to change topics, he contemplated Carmen a moment longer. Then he said, "Thinking is good, Carmen. This is the afterlife, not the army. We want you to think things through for yourself."

Finally some useful information, and pretty well proof that he couldn't hear what she was thinking. Right?

After that, the information he offered about her next Electus was like a giant buzzing of bees in her ear. She tried to concentrate, but at the end, when she was nodding sagely at him as if she'd taken in every piece of information, all she could remember was that her Electus was a young boy. That, and something about his purpose for transition being to draw his parents together, appreciate what they had, and pour their life force into a new baby. Bla bla bla. She was still stuck on the "young boy" part.

"Dogs? Kids? Why do I keep getting the hard ones? Dulcie gets sick people. Lev gets...oh, I don't know what Lev gets." She looked hard at Zeke. "Who chooses the Electi? Is there something you're not telling me, Zeke?"

Zeke shifted uncomfortably. To his credit, his gaze shifted away from Carmen, but his answer didn't help. "It isn't important to know who chooses them, but there is a reason. Now that you're starting to learn about your First Life, and especially, about your special ability here, you'll begin to understand why you're being particularly tested."

"I didn't sign up for a particular test, Zeke." Carmen's words came out choppy and clipped. "I like it here, and I love being a song angel, but I don't want to excel! I don't want to be tested! I just want to do what everyone else is doing…figure out final music, help Befores with their transitions…isn't that enough?"

Zeke scratched that little goatee and adjusted his glasses. Before he could formulate an answer, Carmen was off again.

"Besides, what does this have to do with my First Life?"

"I can only think of two words to say at this point, Carmen." I leaned in. Here it was, the mystery of Electi selection to be revealed in only two words. Awesome.

"Grooming chamber."

Grooming chamber. Groan. No help at all.

On second thought, maybe not such a bad idea.

***

Nope. No weight room in the grooming chamber. But all thoughts of Zeke's muscly arms and how they'd got that way faded in the soft, steady air that whooshed from the tubes on all sides of Carmen and Dulcie.

The grooming chamber was Mezzo's spa; the song angels hung, suspended, as air combed over every part of their bodies. After many trips to the grooming chamber, Carmen had only just gotten over the urge to stare at the air – stare at nothing! – to try to see the powerful hands she could feel, stroking away the grime and kinks that had gathered. Fingers cleaned and groomed her hair, massaged her from scalp to toes, left her feeling better than the best shower ever could on Before. But there was absolutely nothing to be seen. The air in the chamber was alive with invisible fingers that left Carmen feeling like she was in heaven! *Is that okay to say?* And she realized she'd have to be content with that feeling only, not the seeing.

"So... you mean the choice of our Electi has something to do with figuring out our lives on Before?" Dulcie, like Carmen, was still trying to sort out this new information.

"Yup. So says Zeke, who knows everything." Carmen's mind wandered sideways a little. "Hey, Dulce...does your commander know everything? What's her name again?"

"Morgan. And no, she doesn't. She's probably on probation, or something." Dulcie paused, checking her brainwaves for messages from Morgan. It must have been still, for she continued. "She must have been on the wrong website, or got the email mixed up or something, but the last time she assigned me an Electus, she gave me somebody else's. When I got to Before, there were two of us sniffing around this old fellow, sticking tunes in his ears and giving each other dirty looks." It probably hadn't been funny then, but it seemed so now. Dulcie snorted. "It was classic."

Maybe Zeke wasn't so bad after all. At least he could keep the Electi organized.

"My new Electus is a kid, a little boy." Carmen paused, processing ideas as she spoke. Dulcie already knew about Carmen's memories of her First Life starting to surface. "So what's important there? What does this have to do with being a First Life who didn't particularly want a baby brother?"

Dulcie's voice was almost softer than a whisper, when words finally came. "I can't imagine that, Carmen. I'd give anything to be back with my little sister."

Ah, angels did cry. Carmen could see that now. Dulcie continued, "Or even to make her life better, to make her guilt and grief go away so she could go forward. She's only a kid, but she's always sad. I can feel it."

Dulcie's patchy wings fluttered slightly, and Carmen had a glimmer of why they remained patchy. "What happened, Dulcie? Can you tell me?"

"We were walking. It was sunny and fun, like it always was with her. She's the funniest little kid. Her ice cream plopped right off the cone in the middle of the street, but I didn't notice. I wasn't watching, at first. She went back." Here her voice slowed, softened. "I only saw the car at the last second, and all I could do was run and push her away." She stopped. "And it worked. She made it."

"But you didn't."

Dulcie smiled a wet little smile and shook her head. "Well, duh."

"And no music?"

"Elephants playing tubas couldn't have got to me at that point. I just wasn't available," she answered. "And I have a feeling that until I can let her go, I'm stuck in Mezzo."

Carmen nodded slowly. "And until she's well again, you won't be able to?"

Again, a sad smile.

The two song angels leaned into each other a little, their wings brushing together softly. It was very quiet.

They were clean. They were combed. They were massaged, manicured and magnificent.

They should have felt great.

Chapter 10

The boy was small but old for his age, which was eight. He ate a lot of popsicles and rode his bike everywhere, dropping it unceremoniously to the ground at his destination and vaulting off from between the wheels and handlebars he'd so suddenly abandoned.

His name was Elijah.

Carmen perched on his roof and watched him approach the house. She'd had a look at the house already. It was very large. Many-paned windows gazed out over a wide lawn that grew on both sides of the circular driveway. A fountain lay in the driveway curve, with a....what was that weird thing in the middle?...some kind of horned, winged, creepy beast cavorting at its center. An expensive car was parked by the stairs.

From the air, Carmen had been impressed. From the roof, things looked a little different. Strips of paint curled off the walls, waiting for the next rainfall to liberate them. The grass needed a trim, the fountain was waterless, and the car was expensive, but pretty ancient. Spring's blossoms fancied up the neglected trees a little, but that was temporary.

Carmen heard the arguing before the boy did; the woman's shrill voice was bouncing against the man's barks. The moment he heard, Elijah's jaunty stride slowed and his popsicle-smeared face turned back toward his bike, yearning for escape.

He *was* old for his age; he continued up the wide stairs, pumping his arms a little – for energy and courage, Carmen thought. He stopped on the porch, where Carmen had to lean in and down to see over the roof edge. She watched his gaze drop to his bike again, considering, then lift back to the open door.

"I'm home, Mom and Dad!" he called, in an extra-loud-and-cheery voice. Inside, the shouting stopped abruptly, and Elijah entered, closing the door behind him.

Not a good time to work on music. Carmen shifted uncomfortably on the roof edge. Something was definitely not right here. Not just inside the house, but right under her angel bottom.

She lifted it delicately, reaching under to pat her hand along the roof, then along her bottom and wing tips. Her fingers came away covered in black, sticky stuff. Obviously the roof needed work, too.

I don't believe it! What is it with me? She tried to pick it off her fingers and feathers, but it stuck like glue. Feathers were coming out where she pulled; she felt like tonight's chicken dinner. *I can pass through walls but not tar?*

"Forget it," she muttered. "Back to the grooming chamber."

***

Luckily roof tar was no match for the grooming chamber. A little air here, a blast of it there, and Carmen was in flying form again.

She thought about flying right back to her Electus, but it would be impossible to work on his music with his parents fighting.

How long has it been since I left? Fifteen minutes? But was that Before time or Mezzo time? Were they the same? Certainly no watches or clocks here. She glanced down at her wrist, where she suddenly recalled having seen a watch before.

In that weird way of Mezzo music, the moment's background music swelled into the foreground of Carmen's perception. The music was seven kids singing with...was that their mother? They seemed to be wearing curtains. It was familiar to Carmen; she recognized them running and leaping and skipping around a fountain, which was a jazzed-up version of the one at Elijah's house. Before she knew it, Carmen was singing along, describing female deer and sun rays and tea with jam sandwiches. As she felt herself surrendering to the music and the memory, she had a flash: *This music is playing me like a cheesy musical. The music swells, the memory swoops in for the kill. I'll be tap dancing before you know it.*

Just as the dark hallway appeared, Carmen heard a staccato burst of laughter, as if someone hadn't wanted to laugh, but it erupted anyway.

"Zeke?" Carmen said.

Then darkness, and a doorway opened. Carmen knew she was back in memory, and that she was powerless to stop it.

Young Carmen stood alone on a stage, squinting against the stage lights shining in her eyes. Her dress was poofy, her hair carefully smoothed and her shoes shiny. As she opened her mouth to sing, she threw her shoulders back and looked toward the place she knew her family was sitting. The only sound was the occasional squeak of a stacking chair against the gym floor.

The girl closed her eyes and opened her mouth. It was the same song Carmen had just heard in Mezzo - the tea, the deer and the sun rays. Now the audience was completely still, as Carmen created a story with her voice and eyes. The small girl's large voice roamed right to the back of the gym.

Then suddenly there was a noise, and then another noise. Chairs squeaked as people glanced sideways to find its source. On stage, Carmen frowned a little as her eyes darted over the audience. But she kept singing.

Then the noise came again, unmistakable this time. "Carmie! Carmie!" There was a shushing noise. On stage, the girl kept singing, but her posture shifted and her eyes looked downward. Then the noise again, and the scrape of a chair as a woman in the audience lifted a small boy from his chair and swept him up the aisle to the exit. As she hurried away, the boy started to scream the same frenzied word, his arms flailing back toward the stage.

It was hard to hear the song now. The man left in the chair beside the now-empty one watched the woman and boy leave, then rubbed his forehead wearily.

On stage, young Carmen suddenly closed her mouth and turned her back to the audience. Then she walked slowly off the stage.

As the music abruptly ended, there was one loud wail from backstage. "I HATE HIM!"

Carmen could feel the anger of the young girl swirling inside her. From her spiky hair to her wingtips, she seethed with the resentment of having another moment in the spotlight destroyed, however innocently, by a sibling who took so much of her parents' time and attention.

Then she felt a tap, a very gentle tap, on one of those wingtips.

And there was Lev, standing in front of her. His arms were crossed, his forehead was wrinkled in concentration.

"Hi," he said.

"Hi," she answered.

"What are you doing?"

"Not much."

"We need to talk." His voice was low.

"Okay."

Then he turned and flew away. For once, a snappy comeback wasn't necessary.

Not that she would have had one, anyway.

Chapter 11

That whole thing with Lev was disconcerting.

What a good word, disconcerting. She'd noticed that her vocabulary had become much better lately. She suspected subliminal vocabulary lessons in MindSupply, but there was always the possibility that Zeke was trying to upgrade her. A word a day to increase your word power? She listened around in her head carefully, eyes narrowed in concentration; but nope, no laughter, not even a giggle could be heard.

Back to disconcerting: *I am the Queen of the Disconcerted! I've got these memories coming at me thick and fast, I am suddenly able to change feelings with my hands, and I just had an encounter with Lev that was more about asking for my help than it was about trying to kill me. Um, re-kill me.*

She knew that Lev's new attitude was based entirely on her easing those wicked feelings he usually toted around. Would it last?

Too much to think about. Do instead.

***

She found Elijah and his parents at a carnival. Not a the-latest-rides-technology-can-offer carnival. Everything inside the sign over the entrance, a leering clown beckoning you in, had seen better days. But the bright, jagged organ music mostly covered the rides' squeaks and squawks, and the crimson caps almost hid the gray boredom in the eyes of the teenagers operating rides. The air was alive with the shouts of hawkers and the smell of cooking oil; the ground teemed with non-winning tickets and styrofoam cups.

Elijah loved it. Carmen found him on a ride with his dad, zipping at crazy angles through the air, mouth open in soundless delight. Even his dad looked happy, which cheered Carmen. This working with a kid was not going to be easy. If it turned out his life on Before was misery, it would be even worse.

Where's his mom? Carmen floated over the ride, looking around slowly to find a woman who might be Elijah's mother.

Give me a break. That's not her, is it? It can't be. But Elijah was waving crazily at her as he whipped by, at the tired-looking woman with the very large due-pretty-soon belly.

Are you kidding me? How obvious can they possibly be? And just in case Zeke was listening...*I get the baby connection. I get it.*

Carmen dimly heard the hydraulic system dropping the octopus arms of the ride back down to the ground. She watched the little family reunite. She tried to focus, to watch Elijah carefully for clues about his music.

It was hard, really hard, with her head aswirl.

Am I really going to have to work with a sibling thing here? I just want to do my job and leave all that other junk in a pile where I never have to look at it.

Elijah grabbed both parents' hands and pulled them on toward his next ride destination. His dad glanced over at his wife; the look she gave back wasn't exactly heart-warming.

This kid needs me to focus on him, not on me. That's what I'm gonna do. Forget that other Carmen and the opera and that litte brother.

Elijah was stuffing some blue cobwebby stuff into his mouth now. His dad was carefully counting change he'd found in his pocket while his mother rubbed her belly, trying to ease her stretched skin. Carmen looked at them both a little more carefully. Like the house, they stood out in their elegant clothing, but their shoe leather was worn, their cuffs were frayed.

What we need here is an excellent song angel, not a multitasking, distracted space case. I want to stay in Mezzo, anyway. So no more memories. That's it.

There. Decided. Carmen watched Elijah turn his head to listen to a scrap of wild music, and suddenly found it easy to focus her whole attention on this little one, his world, his music, his transition.

Those blue cobwebs were called cotton candy, Carmen recalled. He had it on his lips, fingertips, tip of his nose. A sticky blob had found its way down the front of his white collared shirt. Carmen's remembrance of clothing rules on Before was certainly imperfect, and she'd never known how it worked for boys, but a white collared shirt at a carnival?

Seems like asking for trouble.

Yup. Trouble.

"Elijah, your shirt's a mess. How am I ever going to get that out? I told your father that blue garbage wasn't a good idea..." with another of those looks... "but did he listen?"

Elijah's dad grimaced and leaned in to dab at the blue muck.

"You're only making it worse! Leave it be." Then, with a dramatic sigh, "Pretty soon I'll be home all the time. Then I can work on laundry stains, water plants and burp babies. You can bring home all the money we need for things like new shirts."

Elijah's face looked stricken, eyes darting from his mother to his father, as if he knew what would happen next.

"He didn't need to wear a fancy shirt to a carnival, for God's sake. What are you getting so riled up about? Who's going to see us here?" His voice was loud, getting louder by the second.

"Keep. Your. Voice. Down," she hissed back. "What will people think?"

Now Elijah was looking around desperately, and seemed to find what he was looking for. "Hey, Mom...I need to go the bathroom. Can you come with me?"

Weak, but I guess the poor guy is desperate. Carmen watched as Elijah led his mother off. It had been a long time since she'd seen anyone look that happy about going to the bathroom. His father was left with the blue-stained napkin, muttering about pressure and keeping up with the Joneses.

Carmen made a mental note to find out who the Joneses were. That could be very important. In the meanwhile, Elijah and his mother returned. One of her hands was clutched in Elijah's, and the other was on her stomach, rubbing.

"We have to go home now, Brad," she said. "I can't take any more of this traipsing around. I'm traipsing for two, as the whole world can see."

Brad looked like he might protest, but Elijah immediately blocked the possibility by saying, "Me too. I'm tired of this place."

"And I thought this was such a good idea. Stupid dad, eh?"

Elijah's eyes darted upward, from one parent to the other. "No, it was really great, Dad. I loved it! Really!" Now she looked grumpy. "But I'm just tired now, ok? Okay, Dad? Okay, Mom?"

Carmen watched them walk away, toward the parking lot and the dilapidated car. Elijah had placed himself between them, firmly gripping their hands, even trying to swing their arms back and forth a bit.

Good luck with that, little man.

Carmen felt something stir inside of her, some wisp of a feeling that she tried to ignore. She knew the song angel rules; her job was to find the final piece of music that would lead her Electi to the Sweet Hereafter. It was the kindest, most loving act imaginable, for it ensured that each Electus would have a permanently blissful existence. It was the pinnacle of volunteer work.

But it was work that required detachment. Carmen thought of it as being like a Before surgeon; how could you remove a brain tumor if you were so emotionally attached to your patient that you couldn't slice open their head?

Well, she had to slice open their head and insert, not remove, something. And she couldn't do it if she wanted to put her Electus on her lap and give him a huge hug. She had to stay cool.

But there he was, disappearing from view as he tugged his stiff little arms back and forth, trying to make everybody cheerful. Her last view of him, before they all got in the car, was him rubbing his nose up against his mother's belly, kissing hello to whoever was in there.

Wow. Lucky baby. Carmen was surprised at her own reaction, which she quickly buried. Work. Back to work.

But again, there was no point trying to work on his music now. *What kind of crazy assignment is this, anyway?* Thoughts were landing on her brain like mosquitoes on a fleshy arm. *What will those two do to each other when he isn't around to stop them? How long until his transition? How will it happen?*

There were a couple of thoughts buzzing around in the mix that she wouldn't let land, not even for a moment. But she couldn't deny that they were there.

How can someone that little be old and wise enough to love his outrageous parents, and already love the baby that will take so much of their time away from him?

And even more shocking, and unsong-angel-like: *Could this be a mistake? Does he really have to die?*

Chapter 12

Although she felt sure now that Zeke couldn't hear those dangerous questions, Carmen was spooked at even having them. She flew straight to MindSupply, hoping to wipe the weird thoughts right out of her brain.

The silver trail floated toward her head and the cucumbers appeared, pressing gently against her eyelids. Carmen released herself fully into MindSupply, welcoming the diversion, or education, or whatever it would be this time. Her mind felt totally relaxed.

First came a FLim about Elijah, or rather, about Elijah's parents. *Maybe now I'll find out who those Joneses are.* There was a young man, cute and scrubbed-looking; the resemblance to Elijah was much easier to see than in the weary, angry man Carmen had seen at the carnival. He was honking a raucous car horn outside a scruffy apartment building. In a moment, the front door slammed shut, releasing a smiling girl and almost cutting off a stream of curses from a growly voice inside. She looked back once, then skipped to the car. They kissed.

Carmen wondered what had happened to these two. How had they become the sad pair at the carnival, bickering and grim?

They sat close, planning a future together that had nothing to do with rundown housing or cursing parents. They imagined their home, their wonderful jobs, the children they would cherish; most of all, they talked about being together, having the power as a pair to change the direction their lives had taken so far.

Then Carmen saw bits and pieces of the following years: college, a tiny but joyous wedding ceremony, their thrilled faces as they signed the heavy paperwork to own the house Carmen had seen. Tiny, bouncy signatures below pages and pages and pages of words about money and mortgage and debt. She watched a little further, but by now the real story was clear.

They're so afraid of losing what they have and going back to where they came from, that it's cost them their happiness. And Elijah's.

She thought back to the chirpy couple in the car. It just didn't seem right. Wasn't there any way to fix this?

Just a sec. What was it that Zeke said that day, when he first told me about Elijah being my new Electus? She had been too upset to really listen, worrying about her hands, but there'd been something...something else.

She felt as tired as Elijah's parents had seemed. She ran her hands through her black spikes of hair. A little electricity sparked there, and she ran them through again, as the thought she'd been looking for buzzed its way into her brain.

He said that Elijah's transition would bring his parents together. It was something about them appreciating everything they already have. Then she ran her hands through her hair again, liking the soothing feeling they created as they passed over her scalp.

She brought them down slowly and stared at them, spread full before her. Her hands.

She could fix this with her hands.

***

"Have you ever had an Electus who was really worried about competing with some people called the Joneses? Are they movie stars or royalty or something?"

Sometimes, bouncing ideas off another song angel was about the best thing you could do to solve a problem. And Carmen felt like she had a big one here.

"The Joneses? Nope, never heard of them." Dulcie's curls bounced angelically with her vigorous head shake. As preoccupied as she was, the stray thought again bounced into Carmen's head that Dulcie did make a perfect angel. She had a face too sweet for First Life.

Carmen had already explained about Elijah and his situation. Dulcie's only response had been, "Poor little kid." And then, without any more thought, "Does that make it harder to find his music?"

So there. That was it. Even Dulcie, with her patchy wings and difficult history in Mezzo, knew that an Electus' First Life situation was none of a song angel's business; it was all about finding that music.

I didn't even have a chance to explain my idea, to tell her about my hands.

"Hey, Carmen...don't you think it's weird that everyone close to you – me, your Elijah and even Lev – has this brother-sister thing going on? Do you think somebody's sending you a message?"

Ouch. As she had been so many times in the past, Carmen was reminded that behind Dulcie's angelic face and her difficulties in resolving her own First Life, was a quick mind.

"Yeah, I'd kind of noticed that myself, even though I wouldn't say Lev is close to me." Why had Dulcie said that? She didn't know anything about Carmen seeing Lev in the cemetery on Before and what she'd done with her hands, did she? There wasn't a song angel grapevine she could have heard it on; in general, song angels were much too professional for that. Carmen had considered carefully the idea of telling Dulcie about her hands. In fact, she'd thought long and hard about the wisdom of letting Dulcie in on her secret at all. It might be a little awkward, seeing as Zeke had said her ability was just for struggling song angels, and the struggling song angel she was closest to, and who came to mind immediately, was Dulcie.

"I think you kind of are close, in some funny way. He's nasty with everyone, but he saves some really wicked stuff for you. It's like there's some weird, but really strong, negative attachment."

Before the cemetery, Carmen would have been careful to distance herself from Lev. *It's weird that she said that without knowing anything about what happened on Before, but...she might be right.* Besides, Carmen felt so relieved at Dulcie's simple insistence that finding Elijah's music was the only imperative, that she just grinned at her friend and said, "Who knows?"

Her mind felt freer than it had in a while. Since her question about Elijah's First Life situation had been answered so clearly, she felt there was no point in telling Dulcie about her hands and what they could do right now. Time enough for that later, if at all. Her own First Life memories had slowed down. She hadn't been troubled by them for minutes, days, weeks...who knew how time passed in Mezzo? A while, anyway.

She would find Elijah's music, and help his next life make up for the one he was living right now. Done.

"Let's go for a fly, Dulcie! We haven't done that in...oh, I don't know how long! Let's do it!"

Dulcie's smile was her answer, and off they went.

Chapter 13

The sensation of soaring was one that still thrilled Carmen.

I am so glad that I don't just accept this as part of my new life and job. I absolutely know how cool this is, and I never want to forget that.

Dulcie must feel the same. When Carmen looked over at her, Dulcie was pulsing her wings quickly, letting her body wiggle up and down in the wind as if she were on an amusement ride.

Carmen preferred to glide, completely open-winged, feeling air exactly the temperature of her body slip past her face. She had a quick First Life memory – wow, a positive one! – of lying on her back in the ocean gazing up into the clouds, her arms and legs stretched out and completely relaxed. Air, water, wings, arms…for a moment, it all felt the same. The two Carmens shared one body and mind, for that brief second.

Shake that off! Connections back to First Life weren't what she needed. They only seemed to bring trouble.

She and Dulcie floated over the cerulean world of Mezzo, dimly aware of song angels floating below, of MindSupply when they passed it, of the Fountain's quiet cascade. The air was always smooth and soothing here. It felt good at first, but after a while, a look passed between the two song angels that meant they wanted a little more excitement in their flight. As one, they dipped their wings and headed down to Before.

Here, there was rain, there was wind, there even snow. Carmen recalled her one flight through a world of snowflakes. The heavy gray sky, the white crystals dancing everywhere as they fell, Before muffled and waiting below. She hadn't yet experienced thunder, lightning, a tornado…but she could hardly wait!

It was still spring on the part of Before where Elijah and her previous Electus lived, but a song angel could fly anywhere. She and Dulcie moved towards the south end of the giant ball that was Before. They found trees bursting with crimson, burnt orange and fading gold. They found a world folding in on itself, closing its hands over its head for protection from the coming cold, unlike the other end, where everything green and leafy was arching up toward the sun, welcoming its return. They flew over azure oceans and frosty mountain peaks. From way up high, Before resembled a Science project, a giant rubber ball with gouges filled in with water and mountain ranges globbed on with papier mache. Again Carmen thought how beautiful it was from far away, but how warty it got when you examined it closely.

Clearly both song angels were in the mood for a leisurely fly, watching Before slowly rotating below them in its orderly fashion.

"I guess you won't want to try that scavenger hunt again for a while?" Carmen called into the wind, aiming her voice in Dulcie's direction. Nothing like an angel version of a Before kid's game to bring out the nasty competitive streak you thought you'd completely risen above. Carmen and Dulcie had made a list of Before landmarks that would be easy to find: the Eiffel Tower, the Statue of Liberty, the Great Wall of China were on their list. They'd devised a complicated point system, where the easier the landmark was to see, the less points it was worth.

Dulcie had enjoyed working out all the points and rules, but the game itself wasn't her style. There wasn't anything in Dulcie's personality that had to do with starting blocks and racing, whereas Carmen had ripped around Before gathering points as if her very existence depended on it.

Dulcie smiled lazily. "Nah, I think I'm done with the scavenger hunt," she called back.

They had soared in closer to Before and were now directly over a school playground. The sun, slanting low and directly into the song angels' eyes, made them squint.

"No such thing as Mezzo sunglasses," Carmen muttered. "Too bad." She flew in closer, watching teeter totters move up and down, and merry-go-rounds twirl. Totally unaware, she was floating along watching the scene as if it were a FLim in MindSupply, Dulcie just behind her.

And then she saw the boy. He was young – younger than Carmen's brother would have been - and he had deep brown skin and hair that curled almost to his shoulders. But all the differences in the world couldn't help Carmen keep a safe mental distance when she saw him on the climbing frame.

Carmen's legs, floating behind her while her wings did most of the work, started pumping as if she too, were on the frame.

The boy kept climbing, climbing. Carmen was lost now, watching him. She had no idea where Dulcie was.

"Be careful, be careful," Carmen murmured into the wind. "Please be careful." Her heart was hammering madly, her breath coming in wheezy gasps.

And he was. Miraculously, at least to Carmen, he made it to the top, waving his arms in victory from his high spot.

But not Carmen. That same foot-tripping feeling she'd had so many times before, that same forgetting that she was now an angel clutched her hard, and she could feel her wings slacking, her movement forward halting instantly.

Then she was falling, reeling down towards Before.

Chapter 14

She flipped end over end, wings flapping uselessly, for what seemed like forever. Silence surrounded her. Her eyes were closed.

"CARMEN!"

Her eyes jerked open.

"Use your wings! Now! Flap your wings!" Dulcie's voice, usually so gentle, was loud and harsh, and quickly coming nearer. In a second, Carmen felt Dulcie's small body beneath her. Both were still descending, but the momentum had slowed; the pressure of Dulcie beneath her was slowing her free fall.

The silence around her became sound again, and Before started up below her. She pulled her shoulders back a little and her wings lifted, once more obeying her brain's direction. Pulling upward, she glanced down to see Dulcie coming up after her, flying close to make sure she was going to be okay.

"What was that? What on earth was that?" Dulcie's eyes were wild, her adrenaline rush all used up.

"Not really sure," Carmen mumbled, shifting her eyes away from Dulcie's. She reached out her hand to squeeze her friend's. "But thanks, Dulce. I don't know what would have happened. Would I have fallen all the way through Before and come out the other side? Thanks to you, I don't have to find out."

"I'm just glad I was there. No big deal," Dulcie replied.

Here Carmen angled herself and looked directly into her friend's wide blue eyes. "Actually, it was a big deal. You jumped...well, flew...in and saved me without stopping to think about it, and you did the same for your sister on Before. That is a big deal. A very big one."

Dulcie didn't say anything, just kept flying. And in that instant, even jumbled up inside as she was, Carmen had a sense of what it was that Dulcie needed in order to move into the Sweet Hereafter. She glanced down at her hands, and hoped fervently that she'd be able to figure out how to help her friend do it. Then she abandoned herself again to flying, trying to relax her body back into the glorious state it had been in before her fall.

"Hey, Carmen?" came Dulcie's quiet voice. Sounded like a revelation coming up.

Too tired for this. Want to rest. But she knew she would listen and try to help.

"Did you hear what I said before?"

Did I miss something? What important thing did Dulcie say? I've got to start listening better.

"I said, 'What on earth was that?'" Dulcie said slowly. "I haven't even got First Life out of my vocabulary. Song angels don't call it 'earth'".

Wasn't awareness the first step toward making a change?

"At least you realize it, right? That's got to be a good step." Carmen's eyes ran down the length of Dulcie's patchy wings, then she flexed her hands in the air.

There really wasn't any more to say, so the two song angels headed back to Mezzo.

***

Back and forth, back and forth. It was a good thing all these flights between Before and Mezzo were free. No student transit pass could possibly cover this. But here she was, heading back down to Before, searching out Elijah.

She found him alone at the kitchen table in the old house. The polished wood table already had a couple of nicks out of its surface, but Elijah was taking no chances. He'd carefully placed pages torn from several magazines over the whole surface. Paints and brushes lay scattered beside a shiny black picture frame with spaces for many small photographs. It had been clumsily opened and most of the photos had been removed. Each was a photo of Elijah at a different stage of his younger life.

Elijah was carefully working on a tiny painting of a baby's face. *Blue eyes and brown hair like Elijah, and sucking its thumb.* She angled her head and moved closer to get a better view, and figured that's what it must be. Another picture, drying right on top of the glass and bleeding blue off its edges, was of a large bowl of water with a giant fly standing up in it, and a third one dripping over the frame as it dried showed two tall stick people, their beanpole arms wrapped around each other's skeletal frames.

A little wishful thinking on his parents, Carmen thought as she examined the cuddling stick figures. She looked closely at the fly and water bowl, but couldn't decide what that was. After a moment, she thought she'd better give up on it and work on some music for Elijah, while he was so still and focused.

She started with kid songs and holiday songs, but got no reaction at all. She wondered if those busy parents ever had time to sing with him. Then she tried some classical music, some opera…maybe just the kind of music his parents thought they should all listen to…but again, there was no sign at all that anything special was registering within him, other than the satisfaction of preparing for and loving a baby he'd never even laid eyes on.

Carmen was just shaking off that thought when she heard steps clicking out in the hall. They stopped abruptly when they reached the kitchen door.

"ELIJAH! What is going on in here?"

Carmen's own shoulders drooped in concern, but Elijah's face was luminous as he showed the paintings to his mom.

"For the baby, Mom!" he explained. He wasn't looking at her face – Carmen was – so he kept going. "This is what he'll look like, like me, right? And here's the fountain outside…see, I even put water in it. Maybe we can get it fixed now and I can take care of my brother when he wants to splash in it. An' here's you an' Dad, hugging."

He just kept going, oblivious to his mother's gasp and her eyes widening as she took in the magazines, paint, frame.

"You took that off the wall…you've got to be kidding! Do you know how much that cost, Elijah? And it's supposed to be yours. It had all your pictures in it!"

Elijah's hand had stopped painting, his mouth had stopped moving. He was still, watching his mother's approach.

"Are those my new magazines? The ones off the hall table? They were ten bucks each. The frame has paint all over it…and the glass!"

His voice was wobbly now, not sure of the right thing to say. "It was for the baby, Mom. I wanted him to have some pictures, too. I was gonna put some of mine back in. I don't mind sharing with him."

"Oh, Elijah! Where do you get these weird ideas? What a mess!" He was already scrambling, trying to put pictures back and grab brushes, when he knocked the cup of water over, pouring its contents over the photos and table.

Carmen heard a shriek, and that was all she could take. She couldn't even look at him; she already knew what his face would look like, how his whole body would be simultaneously arching toward and away from the person he loved and dreaded so much. Carmen looked quickly away and started to move sideways through the nearest wall.

She told herself it was because it was once more useless to stick around and try to find his music. But she knew that wasn't the whole story.

She couldn't watch his pain; it was as simple as that. Already somehow he had found his way into whatever heart a song angel had.

And she knew that was trouble.

Chapter 15

Carmen buzzed back into Mezzo, the air crackling around her. As always, music played.

Who do you think you are…God? she raged at herself. *There's a reason why his life is like that. All you need to do is find his music, and leave the bigger picture to a bigger brain.*

What was going on with the music? It seemed somehow different, crawling inside her ears in spite of her grouchy concentration on her feelings for Elijah.

But was her heart listening? *You'd think this whole love thing would be better organized up here. I mean, on Before, your heart could lead you around like a donkey on a chain. You'd think a song angel would be beyond that, as CEO of First Life transitions.*

Aaagghhh! Where is that music coming from? Carmen forced her mind away from her heart and up to her ears. It was choral music, sung in many parts. It was pure and soft, and yet insistent in its need to be heard.

"So beautiful," Carmen murmured, suddenly realizing what was soothing her. She extended her wings and flew slowly toward the sound.

Before her in a tight circle was a group of song angels. Perhaps twenty in number, they sang into the center of the circle, eyes fastened tightly on each other. Carmen saw that Zeke was there. No surprise; of course he'd be good at that, too. But she *was* surprised to see Lev there.

Carmen had known this angel choir existed. She'd been invited numerous times to join, but hadn't felt any interest.

Until now. Somehow she had a sense that the melody, floating in and around her body like a massage, would be even more exhilarating if she was actually helping to produce the sound. Even as she was thinking this, the two song angels nearest her moved over slightly, opening a small gap in the circle. Carmen slid forward into it.

When she opened her mouth, the sound that came out found a perfect place in the melody moving between the angels. Was her voice high? Was it low? It didn't matter. She loved her wings tucked solidly in between the angel wings on either side of her. She loved the energy and peace from without and now, from within.

Her eye caught Zeke's, on her left. His eyes did a little twinkle thing, which she took to mean she was earning valuable Mezzo brownie points by being here.

Then she looked straight ahead into Lev's eyes. For once, he looked completely relaxed. The music seemed to have washed all that pain and resentment clear. He looked back at her and inclined his head forward slightly. There was only the music between them.

It went on and on. Carmen wasn't sure for how long, but it didn't really matter. When it was done, an afterhum resonated powerfully inside her; it was almost a surprise to find that she was still a single entity, able to float free from the circle. Then she noticed part of the circle, specifically Lev, gliding toward her.

"Can I talk to you for a minute?" he asked. The music they'd shared made it all seem perfectly easy and natural.

"Sure thing, Lev," she answered.

They drifted off together. Then after a moment of silence, Lev said, "That hands thing you did on Before. What was that about? What other stuff can you do?"

"Oh, I can rearrange waterfalls and I can…" As jokes went, it was pathetic. Besides, Lev looked relaxed, but serious. This was very important to him.

Carmen tried again. "Does this have something to do with your brother?"

Even as relaxed as he was, Carmen could only imagine the effort Lev was making to allow her, in even the smallest way, into the fortress that was his brother's sacred space. He must really think she could do something miraculous for him to discuss Thaddeus. And who knew? Maybe she could.

"My brother, Thaddeus. You know that we are…were…twins."

Ahhh. Probably identical twins.

"Identical," Lev continued. "We loved mountain biking, hated getting up early, had been using each other's photos in the school yearbook ever since we got to high school."

"I can't imagine being that close to a sibling," Carmen said thoughtfully. "That must have been amazing."

"It was, and it was also…the only way I ever knew how to be. But it was even more than that." Here Lev looked right at her, as if second-guessing his decision to allow someone this near his core. He glanced quickly at her hands, then plunged ahead.

"Thaddeus was everything I wasn't. He could talk to anybody about anything. He'd sit beside an old guy on the bus and know his life story by the time it was our stop. I'd still be thinking about how to say hi. He took the hardest bike trails faster than anyone else dared, charmed teachers into forgetting to give us homework, and sang at the top of his lungs whenever he felt like it."

Carmen watched Lev closely, trying to figure out if this was a good or a bad thing. "You sing too," she said with a smile, remembering their music.

"Yeah, now I do. And in a choir, not dancing down the street with the whole world watching. Everywhere Thaddeus went, it was fun. He was kind of magic that way." Here he stopped and looked away, seeing something that Carmen could not. "I followed along in his wake, and I loved it there. That was where I always thought I'd be, beside this Pied Piper guy who was my brother."

"What were *you* like, Lev? You're just telling me about what you weren't, compared to Thaddeus. Did you listen a lot, and understand what was going on? Were you that kind of guy?" Lev brushed the whole idea away, and was suddenly very quiet. "When the cancer came, at first he was so Thad. He told almost no one, ran around like everything was normal. When his hair fell out because of the chemo he couldn't pretend anymore, so he painted his head different colors. He fought like mad, trying all Mom's crazy remedies, exercising to stay strong, meditating. One day he came home with a tattoo; it showed a hand with the middle finger sticking up and the word cancer in fancy letters. What could our parents say?"

Carmen wanted to shift away, to prevent herself from having to hear what was coming next, but she knew that was impossible.

"Then one day, he just quit. Maybe he was too sick or sore or something else, but he was done. He wasn't like Thad at all then, just some wiped-out guy in my brother's body. He was like that for weeks and weeks. He didn't care what was happening in this world. It was like he was just waiting for a bus to pick him up and take him to the next one."

"But you get it now, right? You know it was meant to happen that way, that a song angel was finding his music all that time?"

His eyes were dull, showing no sign that Lev could use his song angel knowledge on that Before pain.

"He just gave up," came the response. "He didn't care enough about me to fight and fight and fight." His voice was almost inaudible now. "I would have, for him. I would have done anything to stay with him. He was my other half."

Then, in an almost matter-of-fact voice, he said, "So now I'm not whole. I'm only a half, and until I get back to Thaddeus, that's the way I'll stay."

Carmen knew what was coming next, and she looked down desperately at her hands, hoping for a clue of what to say. Nope, just hands, lying limply in her lap.

"So Thaddeus is in the Sweet Hereafter?" was all she could think of. Why was Lev in Mezzo, instead of there with his brother? And, come to think of it, why wasn't he still on Before?

He looked at her curiously, as if that was so obvious that he didn't think he should have to answer. "Uh, yeah." Then, after a moment, "I think I heard a bit of his final piece just before his transition. I didn't know what it was at the time, and I didn't figure out what I had heard until I'd been here a long time, but that's what it was. Apparently that happens once in a while, when two people are extremely close. Like me and Thad."

Still no help from her hands, magical and irritating things that they were.

"Umm..so because he isn't here, you know he's there?"

"Pretty much so. I also just remember the look on his face at the very end. He was listening to something, completely wrapped up in it, reaching for it. His body was still with me, but Thad had his ears on something else."

Lev had stopped talking and was watching Carmen expectantly. Clearly it was her turn to speak.

"So you're trying to get to him in Sweet, right?" She was waiting for inspiration, buying time. "It'll happen, Lev. You're a good song angel, and your commander knows it. It won't be long until you're out of here and on to the Sweet Hereafter."

"Who knows? It's not like there's a list of rules anywhere to tell me what I have to do. It could be tomorrow or it could be next year." He stopped again, watching her. "I can't wait. Can you help me?"

The peace from the music they'd made with the choir was definitely waning. It was time for her to be straight with Lev.

"I don't really know how the hands thing works, Lev," she said. "I instinctively reached toward you that day because I could see how much pain you had. My hands did that, not my head. I don't really get it all." She wasn't looking at him.

"Then can you just let your hands do whatever it is they do, and see what happens? That was the first time I've felt good since...I don't know, since Thad got sick. Well, maybe a few times down there after, but I don't think that counts."

That seemed weird. What was he talking about? No time to deal with that now, though.

"Zeke says it's for helping song angels who are struggling, and that's...uh, that's you, right?" Lev nodded. He looked so hopeful; he had trusted so much.

94

"But I can't." It practically fell out of her mouth, blunt and stupid and sorry. "I don't know what would happen. I can't just start waving my hands around, and hope for the best. Maybe it would make you forget about Thaddeus, or bring him here. Or…I don't know. I just know I can't. At least not yet."

Good thing she'd said that fast, or she would never have been able to say it at all. She ran her hands over her scalp, pulling the hair up into an electric frenzy. Stupid hands. Why couldn't they just stick to hair arranging?

"Please? Just try once? Please?"

"No. I can't." She knew what this was costing Lev, and she couldn't find words to make it feel any better. In fact, she knew she was making it worse, being as blunt as she was being, but couldn't seem to help it.

Lev's face did some Jekyll-and-Hyde thing, going from open and desperate to closed and despising in an eye blink.

"So Princess Carmen has this great gift – something none of the rest of us have – but she's too moronic to know how to use it." Something like icicles or daggers were shooting from his eyes into hers. She wanted to look away, but found it impossible.

"And instead of trying to figure it out, she's busy Dulcie-ing around, shrieking and cackling with that vacant, ditzy excuse for a song angel. You make me want to puke."

He didn't fly away in a huff or a flurry or a tornado. He stretched his wings out wide, and shrank his body within them, disappearing inside their protective cocoon.

Finally, Carmen was the one who had to fly away, and when she looked back, all she could see of Lev was a feathered heart shape, throbbing slowly in the air.

Chapter 16

She flew as far away as a song angel who feels pain in every wing and body part could. Did she want a hammock? MindSupply? The Fountain?

She just hung in the air. No decisions came. She just hung.

And then before her was Zeke. He moved in her direction slowly, arcing one powerful wing around her; it was like a lullaby, like hot chocolate on a cold night.

His kindness opened a floodgate in Carmen. Tears and tears and tears.

After a time, Carmen could tell him what had happened.

"I didn't ask for this gift, Zeke. I don't know how to use it. And now Lev is so angry. And he's not *just* angry. This time, he's in agony because he thought I could fix things for him. "

Zeke just nodded.

"But I can't! Don't you see? This isn't a gift, it's a curse!"

"You did the right thing, not using your hands if you didn't know what the result would be. That was smart and mature." He shifted away a little to see her face better, but kept his wing protectively around her. Carmen didn't mind a bit. *Maybe I should have had an older brother, not a younger one.*

"And Lev's...agony, as you put it, is an ongoing process. He's in Mezzo because of that; you have your own story, as does everyone here. Besides, I wouldn't give up on the idea of helping him. You're just not quite ready to do that yet."

"That's for sure." A couple of not-very-angelic sniffs later, Carmen remembered a question she'd had earlier with Lev.

"Zeke, what happened to Lev on Before after he lost Thaddeus? He said something about feeling okay a few times after Thaddeus died. I didn't really get what he was talking about."

"Because I hope you can help him, I'm going to tell you some of this, Carmen. But only if you agree to a little practice session with your gift afterwards."

Wow. What a deal. This might not be the army, but I somehow doubt I can just say no. Then she remembered the tightly-curled feather ball that had been her last glimpse of Lev, and nodded her head once.

"Lev," Zeke began, "could not handle losing his brother on Before. His parents couldn't reach him, counsellors tried, but he was lost. Before anyone around him knew what was happening, he was using drugs and drinking alcohol like there was no tomorrow."

"Because he didn't want a tomorrow, right?"

"That I don't know. Maybe he just intended to numb himself against the pain of Thaddeus' loss. Maybe it was more than that."

"You mean, you don't know if his transition was accidental or…on purpose?" Carmen sighed heavily. "Either way, when he got here, he must have expected to find his brother?"

"Lev's experience as a newbie was, shall we say, a little less calm than most song angels. He moved through the stages of rediscovering his First Life very quickly, and then began looking for his brother. It wasn't pretty when he realized he wasn't here."

"And ever since then, he's been bucking for a promotion to the Sweet Hereafter by being the perfect song angel."

"Something like that," Zeke said. Then he picked up both her hands, and turned them over, examining them carefully. "Shall we move on now?"

Carmen felt ready.

Zeke began by having her hold her hands close together, then wider apart, feeling for the energy that flowed between her palms and fingertips. She practiced running the energy along her own arms and wings, then tried it out on Zeke. She knew she was working only the purely physical part of her gift. The harder part would be directing her ability purposely for a specific result. Still, it felt good to get some practice at any part of it.

At one point, she found her mind wandering back to Elijah. She understood why, but didn't want to deal with it. His life was a mess; could her hands help?

And then, while Zeke had her practice working with a variety of his thoughts and feelings, she had the briefest of First Life memories. This one, unlike most of the others, was gentle and positive. It slipped into her consciousness and out, leaving a whisper of something completely new to her.

There was the baby…her brother, she now knew. He was lying on a blanket on the floor, his arms and legs boxing with the air in that way that babies have. Opera played in the background. He was gazing right at Carmen, large eyes full of interest and love. She just looked back, enjoying this new sensation.

As the memory passed, she became aware of Zeke eyeing her curiously.

"Wow! That was strong," he said. "So now we know that your hands don't only work with others' feelings. They can work with your own, as well!"

"What do you mean?" Carmen thought she might know, but she wanted to be sure. "What was strong?"

"Whatever you were thinking about, I got such a burst of tenderness from you. It was only there for a minute, while you were off somewhere else. But I definitely felt it." Then he added, "Is that enough for now? I'd better be off."

"Yeah, sure," she said, remembering that this was a very busy angel commander. "Thanks, Zeke. I feel a lot better, about everything."

"You know, I do too." Then he hugged her. Hugged her!

She thought about Lev and her little brother and that feeling she'd had...was that Carmen the girl or the angel? Maybe it didn't matter.

Elijah mattered. And so she set her wings to take her down to Before.

Chapter 17

He was alone, again.

He was still working on the paintings. The picture frame had disappeared – probably cleaned off, reorganized and back on the wall. But Elijah was doggedly painting, this time in the nursery.

Probably hiding from his parents.

A music box, tinkling its tinny, robotic tune, had been carefully placed within reach for rewinding, but not close enough to get covered in paint. Elijah's painting showed a boy climbing stairs, a large H sign, and a baby in a crib.

"The baby's name is Howard? Homer? Hector?" Carmen shook her head. "Don't think his parents will go for those."

The music wound down and stopped. In the silence, Carmen became aware of the sound of voices from downstairs. They were loud and hard. Elijah quickly reached over to wind up the music box again, landing his elbow in blue paint. He wiped it off on his pants. Carmen couldn't help but smile.

"Here's my baby at the hospital. I'm going to see him," he sang along with the box.

H for hospital, not Homer. She watched him paint, sometimes sticking his tongue out to help with his concentration, sometimes holding his forehead in one hand if things weren't going well. He had a lot of paint on his forehead already; things mustn't have been going that well.

"This picture is the story of my brother's life," Elijah said softly. "All the important parts will be here." Carmen didn't want to think about how short Elijah's version of his brother's life might be. Who was in charge here? Who could she talk to?

The music faded again, and the voices below rose. Elijah rubbed his forehead and reached again to rewind the music box.

"I guess I shouldn't just watch him," Carmen thought, although that was exactly what she wanted to do. The more paint he spattered on himself, the more her heart wanted to do a happy dance. He was adorable.

But she ran songs for him, humming them softly in his ear as he spread paint on brush, paper and forehead. She tried slow, soothing lullabies like Twinkle Twinkle Little Star, and zippy ones like The Wheels on the Bus. She even tried running the music box tune through his head, but nothing clicked.

When she had emptied herself of all the tunes she'd collected for him, Carmen hung motionless in the air. Part of her wondered why it was always so difficult to find her Electi's final pieces. Another part didn't really care. She wasn't very committed to the idea of Elijah's transition. The voices downstairs were getting louder; she looked down at her hands.

"It wouldn't hurt anything just to try it once," she told herself. "Nobody has to know." Zeke popped into her mind. Until today, her only concern with being in trouble would have been that Zeke might find out. Now, she didn't want to let him down.

But I don't want to let Elijah down either.

She closed her eyes and moved a little away from Elijah, toward the door from where the sounds came. She rotated her shoulders and dropped her head, then let her hands float free toward the sound. She could feel anger and stress bubbling up from the lower floor of the house, but she could also feel a kind of strangled love.

From Elijah, she got back a wild, panicked love; she added her own angelic benevolence and the feelings she had for Elijah into the mix, just for good measure.

Who knows? It could make poppy seed cake, or it could make Elijah's life better. She hadn't been ready to help Lev, but her session with Zeke had put her that much closer to being in control of this ability.

She kept her eyes squeezed shut, peeking now and then at Elijah to make sure he was okay. It wasn't long before the voices downstairs quietened, and then became murmurs, broken only by the odd female giggle.

Yes! Carmen mind-shouted exultantly. *I did it!* Elijah had moved to the doorway, listening in surprise to his parents' voices. Before Carmen had another moment to enjoy her success, he had clattered down the stairs. Had he heard right? If good things were happening with his parents, he needed to be there.

Carmen and her hands floated up and out, through the roof, through the clouds.

Her mind was busy with two things: how wrong Zeke had been – the gift did work on Before! – and figuring out how next to use it.

Chapter 18

Over the following days, Carmen flew to Before any chance she could get. She had always taken her work seriously, had always been anxious to help each of her Electi as quickly as she could. But this was different. The last time she'd spent this much time on Before was when she was a First Life herself.

Each time she ventured there, she brought music she'd rustled up for Elijah. She told herself that's why she'd come, she hummed each song carefully into his ear as if sure that this was the one. But none of them worked, and she wasn't really surprised; most of the music was pretty lame for an eight-year-old boy. Twinkle Twinkle Little Star? Why had she even bothered? She knew she was risking trouble with Zeke, which suddenly really mattered.

She also knew she was breaking song angel rules, meddling in something that was not her business. But the blaze of joyful feeling that had flooded her when her hands improved the tensions in Elijah's home kept rushing back to her, and she couldn't stand not to try it again.

Maybe I can change his life for him. His mom and dad love each other. They're just really mixed up about what's important. If I can lead them back to each other, maybe they can remember and pick it up from there. She didn't dare voice, even to herself, the idea that there might be some connection between his unhappy home and his nearing transition. If his life improved, might he be spared?

Most shocking of all, Carmen knew that when she looked at Elijah, what she felt was…love. There was no pretending now. She was glad for what seemed like the millionth time that Zeke could only broadcast in her brain, not listen. Imagine him hearing her thoughts about using her hands on Before, about wanting to pick up her Electus and wrap her wings around him so nothing could ever hurt him again. Yikes.

The really strange part was that sometimes when she watched Elijah, his face grew blurry and another face found its way there. This face was her brother's. For both those innocent faces, trusting those older than them to love and protect them, Carmen felt love grow. And as she watched Elijah's unwavering devotion to his unborn sibling, she felt something else, something subtle, shifting inside her.

So while her lips and throat hummed the songs into Elijah's ear, her hands floated up and away from her body, soothing the usually stormy air in the old house. At the very least, the calmer atmosphere soothed Elijah. Carmen thought this would make it easier for him to react to the music she brought him, but she found the opposite. The happier he became, the less attentive he seemed to be to her music. Could this mean that his transition was being postponed, that she really was changing his story? Gradually, over the days that followed, his parents seemed more and more relaxed, more ready to be gentle and accepting of each other.

***

One evening, feeling bold with success, she turned up the energy from her hands several notches, directing it toward the parents. Elijah was in bed, calm and sleepy and adorable. He had finished the set of paintings for his brother. All that was left to do was wait.

Carmen's hands quivered with the energy she unleashed. There was a tiny question mark of doubt in her brain, but she ignored it, and kept the stream of love and hope and good sense flowing down the stairs. She felt fierce and powerful. It wouldn't have surprised her to hear cracks of rumbling thunder or see lightning flashes tear across the sky. Something big was happening here.

At first, when she heard the sharp cry of pain from below, she was startled.

What was that? I expected romantic music, not someone crying. Then came another cry, with a long moan following it. Carmen moved to the top of the staircase and listened, her body completely still.

"The baby," she heard a soft gasp from below. "It's coming, Brad!"

Oops. Lightning, thunder, shmunder. Her hands hadn't brought on a romantic evening...they'd brought on the baby!

Carmen wasn't ready for this. With a soft glance back at Elijah, she fled for Mezzo.

***

Lev was the song angel she saw first. He was not who she needed to see. He was hovering at the center of a group of angels, one of whom was patting his shoulder. All were smiling and nodding. He looked over at her, and it was the old look. Not friendly, not friendly at all. Then she noticed Dulcie at the edge of the group, watching the others. When Dulcie saw her, she flew slowly over to where Carmen was.

It felt good to concentrate on anything other than Elijah. "What's happening, Dulce? Suddenly Lev is Mr. Social, at the center of the pack?"

"I didn't hear it all, Carmen, but I guess he's done something brilliant with his Electus...found some impossible piece in some impossibly short time. You know Lev."

"Yeah, unfortunately." It slipped out before she had time to think. Dulcie smiled, but Carmen felt lousy about her sarcasm. It wasn't actually how she felt anymore. She'd seen too far inside Lev's pain to make fun of the way he protected it.

"Anyway," Dulcie continued, "I guess this will be big points toward Lev getting to Sweet. I know I should feel good for him, but he's such a nasty piece of work. It's hard."

Carmen needed distraction, and she wasn't going to find it in Lev. "Hey Dulcie, do you ever remember seeing angels in churches or famous buildings on Before, floating along on the ceilings with that kind of little smile on their faces? Like the Mona Lisa? Like they knew everything and were still calm and good and wise?"

"Yeah," Dulcie mused. "I think 'angelic' is the word you're looking for."

"Yes! Exactly. Angelic smiles." Carmen could manage a smile, but not a laugh. Even back in Mezzo, she couldn't help remembering that somewhere on Before, a baby was being born right now because of her and her hands. And who knew how that would affect Elijah?

Dulcie's delicate blonde curls were starting to jiggle with the first giggle. "Who knew that angels had..." – giggles turned to a gasping wheeze - "...fashion issues..."

Carmen was laughing now too, in spite of herself. She knew Lev was watching, and she knew what he thought about her wasting time while her gift was left untested. But then, he hadn't been with her just now on Before, had he?

Carmen turned her back on Lev's look and let herself laugh with Dulcie. "Yeah…and…chocolate cravings…" – the laughter felt so, so good – "…and engine failure!" The last word was a howl, and in spite of the puzzled looks of the song angels around Lev and Lev's slowly curling lip, Dulcie and Carmen laughed on and on, forgetting about everything they needed to forget.

Chapter 19

Unfortunately, you couldn't forget stuff like that for long. They laughed until they couldn't wring any more tee-hees out of it, wiped their eyes, then looked at each other for a long moment.

"What's up, Carmen? I can see that something's bugging you." Dulcie was like that sometimes…a little bit of angelic sixth sense. Maybe a better gift than magical, out-of-control hands?

Dulcie rubbed pale fingers up and down her patchy wings, her smile as sweet as any ceiling angel. "Carmen?" she asked again.

"Oh…nothing," Carmen said slowly. She knew Dulcie wouldn't buy it, but she also knew she wouldn't press the point. It was too much to explain right now, too weird and complicated. Carmen looked at her hands. She'd barely got used to having wings, and now she had hands exploding with power. The whole upper appendage area was thrilling and troubling.

She became aware of Dulcie's steady gaze.

"Has anyone ever told you what a perfect angel you make?" Carmen said to her friend, in a sudden rush of words. "You were made to be an angel."

Dulcie wasn't fooled; no doubt she knew that Carmen was changing the subject to avoid a discussion, but she went along with it, just as Carmen had known she would. "It's kind of weird that you say that," she said, "'cuz my grandma used to tell me all the time that I looked like 'a perfect little angel'. She even had a picture of me in the hall – no one else, just me! – that she called 'my angelic Dulcie'." Dulcie's eyes had that faraway look that Carmen knew so well, but this time, for such a different reason. "I kind of wish that she could see me now...or that I could see her."

The picture in Marion's hall. The picture of the angel who had reminded her so much of Dulcie.

No, not possible.

Carmen was exhausted, beyond the point of properly registering one more surprise. "Your grandmother would be proud, Dulce. Look, I gotta go. I need to do something, ok?" Carmen didn't even know what it was, but she knew that time was ticking along on Before, bringing babies and whatever else might come with them. Dulcie nodded, then began rubbing her wings again, as if she were cold.

Carmen gave her a hug, then spread her wings.

One thing was certain. When this was all done, she was going to use her hands to help her friend. Dulcie, who had bound herself with steel heartstrings to her suffering sister on Before, who didn't think she deserved thanks for risking her own neck to save Carmen's, whose patchy wings told her whole painful story.

Carmen floated along, letting her wings lead, leaving her mind blank. She heard a melody in the distance, voices blending in a way that made the usual background music of Mezzo fade to gray. She let her ears guide her toward it; the choir had gathered near the Fountain. The Fountain's rising and falling – today in silver and greens – filled her eyes, while the music caressed her ears.

She folded her wings and tucked herself neatly between a tall, dark-skinned song angel and a graybearded one, feeling the song rising up in her throat, like the first time. She opened her mouth and let the music pour out. This time it was opera – Carmen recognized it easily now – and some part of the First Life self still glowing inside her drew energy and peace from the music. She avoided looking at Zeke, although she knew he was there. She had that weird someone's-staring-at-you feeling, and she was pretty sure who it would be.

The opera music drew her in even more quickly than other music did. It drew her so far in and so fast, that it took a moment for her to register that her body might still be amongst the other song angels, but her head was now somewhere else.

Her mind was in her home on Before, in the living room. Moonlight streamed in through the open curtains. The music poured forth, whirling and twirling from the speakers so the room lay pulsing in its power. There lay her mother and father, face up on the soft carpet, eyes closed. Carmen lay between them. No brother in sight. Carmen found herself looking around for him expectantly, wanting to see him again. But he wasn't there.

Carmen watched herself, snuggled tight between her parents, serene in their love for the music and for her.

Then came a call, and the sounds of small feet plopping down a hallway. Her brother appeared in the doorway, hair sleep-tousled and dragging a blanket. The girl squeezed her eyes shut, tried to hold on to each parent's hand so neither could escape. Gently, the man extricated his hand and got up to bring his son into the group. The girl's face sloped into a pout; the angel felt impatient with her nonsense.

The music suddenly dropped and became quiet, almost a whisper of song. It was the clown song again. The clown had been hurt, badly hurt, but he had no choice but to climb back into his costume and pretend to be happy. It was his job to make others smile, even if his own heart was broken.

And now Carmen saw herself at a playground, with her brother. They were both older now. Carmen wore jeans with ripped knees and earbuds plugged her communication with all but her music device. Her brother was wiry and athletic, with scabs on both knees to prove his bravery. They were on their own this time.

"Watch out on that climbing frame, okay? The last thing I need is more drama about one of your accidents." The girl barely looked at her brother as he started to climb. She gazed intently at her device, searching out one song after the other.

So she didn't see him climb high, hand over hand, occasionally stopping to wipe the sweat from his palms onto his grimy shorts. He hung from the bars by his hands, then swung his legs up to hang upside down. She didn't see him swing lazily there, looking over at her. He called her once, but her music was too loud.

And the girl didn't see him flip back up and grab for the top bar. Miss that bar. And fall sideways, hard, against the frame. The scream was immediate, as was the blood. Carmen the angel could see it, but the girl did not. It was only after a nearby parent shook her roughly on the shoulder that she looked up and saw a crowd of bodies around the climbing frame, and saw that one body, her brother's, was so obviously missing from his usual spot at the top.

Then she was up, in a flash. She dropped her music, flew in amongst the bodies just as the ambulance siren started to wail. Now it was the girl's turn to scream.

Carmen the song angel pulled back and turned her head away. Just then, the opera music floated back, brought her safely to her spot within the song angel choir. Her body was still, releasing the last notes from a calm throat. Her mind was chaos.

What a brat! She deserves to feel horrible. Why wasn't she watching him better? Why would she do that to her brother? To her family? And then, *Why would I do that to my family?*

She could feel a space widening between the girl Carmen and herself. It was painful, like peeling off little sections of her skin one chunk at a time, but it felt good, at the same time. She glanced around at the angels near her; no one seemed to notice her turmoil. She didn't even peek in Zeke's direction. The last thing she wanted to do was have a Zeke chat.

She flexed her wings quickly, readying for flight.

"Carmen, we need to talk." Zeke. Uh-oh. Carmen felt her stomach tighten. Was this going to be about what she thought it was going to be about? It had felt so right to help Elijah's parents; now she was afraid of the consequences, and afraid to justify herself to Zeke.

"You shouldn't be here right now. Your place is on Before, with your Electus. Things have changed there for him." *Ahhh…here it comes. And why have they changed?*

"His brother has come, and his own time is coming. Your Electus needs his final piece, Carmen."

He didn't know! He didn't know what she'd been doing with her hands; he didn't even know that she'd changed the need for Elijah to leave Before!

But what a mess. She'd fooled Zeke…but that was okay, wasn't it? It was for a good reason. What was that saying about the end justifying the means? Didn't her sorting out that situation on Before justify the little issue with using her hands, even if it was against the rules?

She liked Zeke. She admired him, even. She wanted him to be proud of her, and the only way that would happen now was if she kept quiet about what she'd been up to.

Lied was a better word for it.

"I'm sorry, Zeke…you're right. I should be on Before, helping my Electus," she mumbled. Helping him how? She left that part out, and instead focused her eyes on his eyebrows, hoping to avoid actual eye contact. Then before she knew it, and without actual permission from her brain, her mouth blurted out, "You've got it totally together, Zeke. I'm sure you were oozing serenity and wisdom when you flopped out of the Fountain, right?"

His eyes – even though she wasn't looking directly at them – widened as he answered, "Well actually, no. If I had it all together I would be in the Sweet Hereafter instead of Mezzo, right?"

"Really?" Wow…not what she had expected at all. "I just thought you were kind of slumming it, that you could go there anytime but were working here to help out."

The eyebrows she was still staring at raised up. They raised up quite high.

"Sort of like volunteer hours?" Zeke said. Was he teasing her? Better not be. "No, Carmen. I'm here for the same reason you are. I'm not quite done with Before." As the eyebrows dropped down to their usual position, he added, "I'd like to tell you about it sometime."

Wow…Zeke wanted to confide in her, tell her his innermost secrets, his deepest, darkest…

"It *is* important to question things, think about things, and work them out for yourself, Carmen. *I* like it. *God* likes it. Now - get going!"

She wanted to hug him. Was this how it would have felt to have a big brother?

She turned toward Before and opened her wings, smiling at Zeke. She felt so much better!

But as she neared the diseased oak tree that marked the beginning of Elijah's driveway, she knew that something wasn't quite right. She just couldn't put her finger on it.

It wasn't until she'd circled Elijah's house a couple of times and started her landing that she realized what it was.

Oh my God.

She had never said aloud…not to anyone…that she wondered if Zeke and his higher ups – notably God – would approve of her questioning the rules of Mezzo. She'd only thought it. So that meant… ChannelZeke wasn't just a transmitter. He was a receiver, too.

Zeke knew exactly what she was up to, because he could hear every one of her thoughts.

Oh my God.

Chapter 20

Did Zeke approve of her…um…unusual approach with Elijah? Was Mezzo really that stretchy about the rules? Did he think what she had been trying to do was impossible? Then he hadn't seen the change in Elijah's parents. Or was he waiting for her to fall flat on her face?

Don't know, and don't care right now, came the thought as she made a quick check of the rooms. She'd known the minute she entered Elijah's house that it was empty, but checking through each room postponed the moment she had to go to the hospital, the moment she had to pretend to try more music that she knew Elijah would never need. She could feel Zeke in her head now; it felt full to bursting. Was he located in a couple of the gray wriggly-worms that made up her brain – in that case, if only she could rip those few out – or was he tossed, like a shroud, over the whole thing?

I can't believe I ever thought it was just me in here. Lev is right, I am a hopeless case.

ChannelZeke was silent. Silent, but there.

Carmen floated to the baby's room. Elijah's paintings were arranged in a row along the wall, down low at a child's eye level. Carmen sat cross-legged before them, looking at each one carefully. There were several more than there had been the day he'd started. There were the ones of the baby's face, the fountain, the cuddling stick parents, but now also ones of Elijah and the baby, and of the baby in front of a Christmas tree, an angel looking down from the treetop. The last painting showed two adults and a baby, cuddled together; it seemed strange to Carmen that Elijah hadn't painted himself into the family portrait.

It's like a mini storybook of the baby's life. Like a lifechain, like a quilt. The paintings reminded Carmen of the squares in the quilts of her grandmother and Marion, patiently stitched to include the moments of sadness and joy that made up a life, and they were like the lifechain whose pendant represented the overarching story of an angel's Before life and death. Suddenly, Carmen knew she needed to meet Elijah's baby. She knew that meant going to the hospital, which somehow didn't feel good. But there was no choice.

She found the hospital; some kind of angel instinct led her there. *How come I can do that, but can't tell my own brain has a population problem?* She could still feel Zeke there. There was an ominous sense of waiting inside her head. Waiting, and something else.

Carmen entered cautiously, trying to understand the sick feeling in the pit of her stomach. She flew hesitantly, waiting for answers, or even for the right question. She found both when she turned a corner and a door opened suddenly in front of her. Out came a nurse, walking slowly beside a girl whose legs were bound by braces. The girl propelled herself along on crutches. She seemed to be new to it, and it looked like hard work.

Carmen didn't need a memory, with or without opera soundtrack, to tell her why she hated the hospital. She remembered being in the hospital where they'd taken her brother by ambulance after the fall, and she remembered being there weeks and months later, as he gradually gained strength. Her whole First Life lay suddenly before her, without doors or hallways or music. She remembered her mother seeing her son for the first time after he fell, and she remembered the first time her brother saw the leg braces he would wear for the rest of his life. She knew that all their lives changed that day, and felt, no matter what anyone said, that it was her fault. If she'd watched him better, it wouldn't have happened.

The truth was that it *was* her fault, and there was no getting around the truth. That lived inside her every single day of her life after that. When her brother cried because his legs hurt, she remembered. When he saw his friends heading for the soccer field and threw his crutches aside in frustration, she remembered.

And now Carmen the song angel remembered the day it became too much to live with. She could feel both the relief and the despair that came with the idea of leaving Before, but one day, it became the only option for her. So she said silent goodbyes to the family she loved more than anything, but had failed. She grabbed her music and her earbuds, and headed for the subway. The closer she got, the clearer her mind.

And then came the cold. The flight. The nothing.

Carmen floated away from the girl with the leg braces. She needed to keep moving. She found the floor, the corridor, the room. She floated through the wall like nothing and hung at the room's edge, away from the bed where the woman lay, resting, smiling. Her husband had pulled a chair close to the bed and was holding her hand, stroking her forehead. Elijah had maneuvered himself right between them, and everyone looked good with that.

Carmen's heart felt peaceful. She hoped Zeke was watching this now, that he could see what her work had done. The baby was here, Elijah was happy and loved. This family of four was working out perfectly.

"But you just saw the baby, Elijah. We went to the nursery before we came here," said his father.

"I know, Dad," Elijah answered. "But then I wanted to hurry to see Mom, that she was okay."

"What a great big brother you'll be, Elijah," his mom said. "I know you'll take good care of our baby."

Elijah threw his arms around his mom, and then said, "But can we go see him again, Dad, and then come right back? What if he's crying or something?"

"Just two seconds, buddy. I just want to make sure Mom is falling asleep before we go, okay?"

So Elijah had to wait. Carmen watched him wiggle out from between his parents, rub his forehead, then move toward the window for a little look.

"Dad?" he tried again. But his dad's eyes didn't move off his mother's eyes, and those eyes didn't seem to be closing at all. Elijah glanced towards the door, a few steps away.

Slowly he started edging his way there, one silent footstep at a time. Carmen could only watch him. Her hands were powerless.

The door opened with a quiet hospital hiss; it wasn't enough to disturb Elijah's parents, lost in their happiness. Elijah was out, and on his way to the nursery. All Carmen could do was fly behind.

He headed down one hall, glanced at an elevator, and then moved into a nearby stairway. He angled away from voices and sounds, keeping to the darker stairs and halls that would protect his flight.

"I have to hurry," Carmen heard him whisper as he started down the echoey staircase. "I think he might be crying."

He poked his head from the doorway to check for people before stepping out, then travelled another corridor to another flight of stairs.

This stairway seemed very cold and very dark. Elijah stopped at the top of the stairs, his eyes squinting as he tried to remember the way back to the nursery.

He was getting tired. And Carmen could only watch.

Chapter 21

"Did we come up these stairs?" Elijah's uncertain voice reverberated in the quiet staircase. It was many, many flights down.

"I remember there was a big clown statue at the very bottom," he said. "I 'member 'cuz I don't like them." He was up on his tiptoes, trying to angle his head to see what lay at the bottom of the many flights of deserted stairs. "They pretend to be happy, but really, they're sad." Even on tiptoes, he couldn't see down far enough, so he climbed onto the bottom rung of the iron railing. "And sometimes they're mad or mean."

Carmen was floating, fluttering as near to Elijah as she could. Her hands were stretching out to him, her wings beating the air as fast as she could, creating a wind to push him safely back to the landing.

But Elijah was leaning over the top ledge of the railing, almost able to see what lay at the bottom. "When I get to the bottom, I will run by that clown with my eyes closed, so he doesn't see me." He balanced atop the ledge, holding on firmly with both strong little hands. "Why is it so weird windy in here? I don't even see a window." One more little peek down. "It feels like flying up here, in this wind and cold."

Just then the door behind him opened, and his father came through it. The name he'd been about to call stuck in his throat as he saw Elijah, and he reached, lunged for his son hanging over the railing.

Too late. Elijah gave one more tiny push against the wind, eyes fixed downward.

He thought he could hear music. Then only cold. Flight.

Nothing.

Chapter 22

And in that moment, Carmen knew she had a choice to make. She now knew…everything. But none of it mattered. All that mattered was Elijah and his music.

For the gap of time between heartbeats, Carmen imagined a life with Elijah in Mezzo. She loved him. She was ready to take care of a little brother. At long last, she was ready. And without his final piece, Mezzo would become his home.

It was meant to be this way! That's why I couldn't find his music.

And just then, the music came to her. The carnival music was Elijah's final piece. Carmen knew it. Loud calliope music, notes wheeling crazily up and down the scale.

Below her, Elijah's father was leaping down the staircase, swinging wildly from one set of stairs to the next. He was sobbing. Doorways were opening, and there were voices coming, and agony to follow. Floating down the staircase, she saw Elijah, broken and still, at the bottom.

Suddenly, he eased up and rubbed his forehead in confusion, much as he had done moments earlier in the hospital room. Of course, all the First Lives could see was a lifeless form at the foot of the clown statue.

Still, Carmen just watched. She held the raucous music in her head and did not let one single note escape in the boy's direction.

Elijah, still dazed, found the other stairs, the ones leading to his next home. He started the climb.

Carmen felt herself lifting, leaving Before. Being lifted, was more like it. She was far above Before now, watching Elijah on the staircase up to Mezzo.

His wings. They're sprouting…he's almost a song angel, he's coming to me. Carmen felt a shock of joy grip her. She tried to eradicate the music, but it would not go. The ear-splitting jangle banged in her brain, hammered against everything inside her. It was trying to get out, to reach Elijah.

She would not let it. She could keep it inside her. Zeke was there, probably waiting like a thundercloud. But right now, it didn't matter. She would sort that out later. Getting Elijah to Mezzo was all that mattered.

The wings opened a little more, the little feet actually lifted off the stairs. His face looked… angelic. There was no other word for it. He had only been a song angel for seconds, but already he was learning the ropes. He was smiling softly and in her direction. He didn't know her yet, but he must feel the love that was waiting for him.

The music tore at her, trying to find Elijah.

She loved him. She loved this boy with all her heart; her Before heart, her song angel heart.

She waited. Zeke waited.

But as Elijah climbed the stairs near where she hung in the air, she knew the truth.

She was going to let him go.

She would happily die – again – holding that music inside, but that wouldn't be what Elijah deserved. He deserved, at the very least, the Sweet Hereafter.

Carmen let the music flee her body. It exited from every pore and feather on her, flew in true carnival jangle to find Elijah. He heard it, felt it, and stopped on the stairs, confused. He stood still, listening, his face bewildered. His wings were slowly folding up. And then the bewilderment began to disappear from his face, just as his wings resettled back into his body, becoming only shoulders again.

He rubbed his back and shook his head, then started to climb upwards. His legs were in control once more, with only a twitch of movement from his shoulders to indicate what might have been. His power to move shifted once and for all from shoulder to shin.

Like a leering clown gone murderous, the tacky, horrible carnival music screamed on, pounding out its fury at having almost been ignored. Carmen let it attack her; nothing could feel worse on the outside than what was happening to her heart on the inside.

Elijah had climbed past her when he stopped suddenly and looked back. His hand reached out behind him, groping for something he could feel, but not see. He was smiling.

Go. Go. It was all she could think. Her heart was splintering. She watched his ascent until her eyes lost him in the brilliant light.

The music ceased instantly. All around her was darkness.

Carmen felt the darkness enter her and then everything was black.

Chapter 23

She knew that Zeke had come down for her, folding her gently inside his powerful wings, carrying her back to Mezzo. She knew that he was purposely trying to stay off ChannelZeke, to give her time to mend and think in private. Every once in a while she'd sense him there, but like he was dipping his finger into the water that was her, making sure she was okay, and then disappearing.

After a while, she *was* okay. At first, she spent a lot of time at MindSupply, watching FLims about the Gobi Desert and driving etiquette in Japan and how to tell a frog from a toad. None of it was useful, but that was exactly why it was so useful. She needed to forget, even for a little while. Whenever a FLim topic veered anywhere near babies or opera or water color painting, it was dismissed. Once, when the strains of raucous calliope music oozed into her ears before she had a chance to read the title, "The Modern Day Carnival", the green discs barely escaped being ripped off the silver thread.

She remembered how she'd felt about Dulcie's far-off gaze, and wondered if she had the same expression now.

No new Electus was assigned to her; she slept, watched FLims, spent time at the Fountain. Dulcie was often around. Carmen knew she was being watched over, but was usually too weary to say thank you or even to talk.

Even Lev came by. Her silence seemed to urge him to speak; he told her that finding the difficult final piece for his last Electus had put him close to being promoted to the Sweet Hereafter. He felt he was a hair's breadth away from getting there. But he wasn't bragging or goading. In fact, he said that now that he was so close, his need to see Thaddeus had sharply diminished.

"It will be so good to see him, but I've finally realized I'm a whole person all on my own." He looked carefully at Carmen. "I still want him, but I don't need him anymore, princess." How different that word sounded now…almost a friendly nickname.

***

At first, there was no thinking about Elijah. Then, bit by bit, he crawled his little-boy way back into her mind. There was too much to think about. Just the feeling that she had failed him by not preventing his transition was hard enough; then losing him to the Sweet Hereafter, even though she knew that had been the right choice, was like acid trickled over her wound.

Once, when these thoughts were rolling through her mind for the thousandth time, she heard a voice. Its tone was so hesitant that it was hard to believe that it was confident, knowing Zeke. All she heard was, "His transition was necessary for his family's existence. His purpose was always to pull his parents together in readiness for the son who would live out his life with them." So then she knew. It had all been happening in spite of her hands, not because of them. Elijah had been the magic, not her. There was a little Zeke P.S. "I believe I mentioned that your gift was for use in Mezzo only?" Yeah, yeah, yeah.

Slowly, she could let herself think about his gap-toothed smile and that freckled nose, poised barely above the untidy painting of his baby brother. As before, sometimes his face lost definition and Carmen couldn't tell who she was grieving for – Elijah, her brother, or both.

One day she found herself telling Dulcie a story about Elijah. The next, she started talking silently to Zeke in her head without even thinking about it, or hating it. She was talking about her brother, about how sad she felt to be missing his growing up.

She wondered how Elijah was doing. She wondered how her brother was doing. But she knew something was easing inside her, finding some distance from those boys, and though that made her sad too, she knew it was what needed to happen.

So when Zeke came to find her instead of just speaking inside her mind, she wasn't really surprised. She'd had a feeling about it. She looked at Zeke, muscly, goateed, wonderful Zeke, and waited.

Because of recent developments...bla bla bla... coming to terms with First Life...jealousy of sibling...bla...selfish pain caused parents...bla... "and the experience with your most recent Electus, where you showed greater than expected devotion in trying to improve his life, and successfully resisted an enormous temptation to keep him with you in Mezzo instead of moving ahead to the Sweet Hereafter." Here Zeke paused, looking like he wished he didn't have to say what he was about to say.

"Because of all this, your time in Mezzo is deemed over. You are free to leave, and begin your everlasting phase in the Sweet Hereafter."

Carmen had had a feeling, but still, it whooshed all the air out of her. Mezzo...done! The last time she'd changed worlds, there'd been no warning, no time to think about it. It was teeter, fall and rise before she had the slightest notion of what she was doing.

Wow. No more rushing around trying to find the right music for a bunch of First Lives. No more ChannelZeke, no more crazy hands taking control of her life, no more baaaad outfits…here she looked down at the hated garb, then decided she'd better take that one back. Who knew what they wore in the Sweet Hereafter. Ponchos? Velour track suits?

What about the things I got wrong in Mezzo, though? Using my hands on First Lives, and even considering not giving a final piece to an Electus? How weird, thinking this stuff with Zeke beside me. But she did. No military arrests here. *This really is a cool place. Thinking for yourself definitely welcomed, along with the sometimes-nasty results of doing so.*

Her heart, so recently battered over Elijah, now felt ahead to the loss of Dulcie and Zeke. No doubt Lev would be in Sweet soon, which seemed good; she thought she might miss even him.

Zeke was watching her, probably tumbling along with the roller coaster ride inside her head. She wondered again about his Before issue – what could possibly be keeping wise Zeke in Mezzo?

He wasn't saying. "I'll meet you by the Fountain after you've seen Dulcie, okay? Don't be too long." *I guess I'll never know.*

She smiled a sad smile, and let one more thought slide through her brain. Then she waited for Zeke to respond, for old times' sake.

"No, Carmen. No bag to pack, no paper to cancel…very funny."

It didn't help to smile, but they both pretended it did.

Chapter 24

It didn't take long to find Dulcie...MindSupply again. There were tears and hugs, and speculation about new clothing possibilities in the Sweet Hereafter.

"Your lifechain, Carmen! You're finally going to find out what it is! Aren't you excited?" Dulcie said, her voice wobbling.

"Yeah, I guess so," was all Carmen could come up with.

They flew slowly toward the Fountain, their wings and brains in unison. They knew it was their last flight together. Even when they met someday in the Sweet Hereafter, there would probably be no flying.

"Do ya think they're walking around up there? Is that practical? Maybe...hot air balloons?" Dulcie took a last stab at their goofy routine.

Carmen could hardly wring out a response, looking at her friend's sweet face and patchy, tender-looking wings. What she thought was, *With those wings, I won't be seeing Dulcie for a while*; what she said was, "Ride 'em, cloudy!" Possibly her worst pun ever, but appropriate, given that all she could really think about was taking her hands and their gift out of Dulcie's reach, so her friend would have to continue her difficult journey all on her own. Would her hands have any power in Sweet? But then, you didn't get there until your issues were gone, so there'd be no one to help, even if she still had the power.

She could feel Zeke inside her head, listening, and realized that she was dreading the feeling of Channel Zeke slipping away at some point on her ascent of the staircase.

"Maybe I can use my hands to polish halos now?" she said, turning to him. She saw that Lev had shown up behind Zeke. Both Dulcie and Lev looked a little confused, but Zeke just rolled his eyes.

She thought about it, then gave Lev a quick hug. He didn't pull away. Dulcie was hard to let go of, but Carmen finally did. Then Zeke pulled her in to an angel bear hug; she pulled herself away before she could get lost in the protection of those wings.

"Thanks, Zeke." He nodded.

She turned her back on the three, then placed one foot on the staircase. One step, two. Then she turned back. "Keep your eye on the pendant, Dulce. Tell me what's happening back there."

Three, four. She could feel a change behind her, as if a mosquito was traipsing lightly between her shoulder blades, waiting to pounce. She could also feel a change inside her, something she couldn't quite put her finger on. One thing at a time. "Dulcie?" she called over her shoulder.

"I'm watching! I'm watching! It's…" Her voice trailed away just as Carmen felt the mosquito stop. There was a wiggle, and some tiny pressure. "It's a baby, Carmen," came the whisper. "Of course, it's a baby."

What else? Carmen thought the feeling inside would go now, the mystery of her lifechain being solved, but it didn't. It swelled from her heart into her brain, from her wingtips to her fingertips. She tried to pretend it wasn't there. She kept climbing.

She wanted to look back again, but didn't. That would certainly be the end. The next step, and the next.

She was halfway up before the weight of what she was doing stopped her, prevented her legs from pulling her leaden feet up even one more stair. Now she turned to the three, still watching below. The pendant on her lifechain was fully formed and unlocked, but still there; she felt for her wings. Still there too.

It wasn't too late.

She held out one hand, then both, towards the three below. She looked at those hands, and at the song angels floating beneath her, framed by her trembling fingers. Then she slowly started back down the stairs, feeling the pressure evaporating from within her with each downward step.

Fourth step, third, second…she stood in front of them. If Zeke was hearing any of her thoughts in his head, he was ignoring them, waiting for her to tell him what was happening.

"I'm not going."

"You're…not…going?" Zeke spoke the words as if he was learning another language, imitating sounds with no understanding of what he was saying. Dulcie and Lev gaped. Everybody *went*! It was how things worked here.

"No. I want to stay. I want to stay and use my hands, and be a song angel, and help First Lives. I want to be the best song angel there ever was, and…." She looked quickly at Dulcie, then continued, "I want to help Dulcie, and…you, Zeke."

"Are there *any* rules you follow?" flashed into her head, courtesy of Zeke. When she replied, *I'm workin' on that!* right back, she could tell by Zeke's face that he hadn't meant to send her that message. But his eyes were smiling just a little, now. "I'll have to check on this, Carmen. Never even heard of it; I'll have to make a call to the top."

So he turned his back, and over the next minutes said nothing, just gestured with his hands, wiggled his wings, turned back to look at Carmen a couple of times and raise his eyebrows. Carmen felt sweaty for the first time in her angelic life. Lev and Dulcie were looking at her like she was the most wonderful crazy angel they'd ever known.

"Okay." Zeke finally turned around. "It's weird, but upstairs likes your motivation and thinks you have something to offer. So that's all cleared. The tricky part is that things have been set in motion for you to go to the Sweet Hereafter, and that can't be changed. Someone has to go."

Heads didn't move. Only eyes moved. Dulcie looked up, deep in thought. Lev looked down, grinning slightly...crazy Carmen! Zeke looked straight ahead, pulling on his goatee. Carmen looked at Lev, at Dulcie, at Zeke...then back to Lev.

"Lev can go instead of me."

"Carmen! You can't just decide these things. Whether you know it or not, there's some sort of organization here beyond *you*...or had you missed out on that little detail?"

Lev had gone back to gaping.

"No, really. Lev's almost there – just a hair's breadth away, right, Lev? He wants to go, and he's done the work. He's finished here! I'm not."

Zeke's eyes and head and shoulders all rolled back, but he decided against speech. He turned around again. More hand movements, more wing wiggles. One large groan, then silence. He turned back.

"The word from the top is...thumbs up."

"Uh, thumbs up?" said Lev.

"Yeah, thumbs up. As in good, fine, go for it, permission granted."

"You mean he can go? I can stay? It's all cleared?" Carmen whispered.

Zeke just nodded. Dulcie danced up and down the bottom stairs, throwing her arms in the air. Carmen watched Lev.

"Thumbs up? The top says things like 'thumbs up'?" Lev smiled, his face creasing from ear to ear, right at Carmen. "Thumbs up!"

They had said goodbye once, but they did it again. Lev's commander was there instantly, and had a few last words with him. She could see from their interaction that not everyone had Zeke's big brotherly way; she inched closer to Zeke, even more sure that she had made the right choice.

And then it was time…again. Lev hugged Dulcie – whose eyes bugged out – and nodded a smile to Zeke. Carmen waited for him at the bottom of the staircase.

"Did I ever tell you what my name means, Carmen?" He laughed, before she could answer. "Of course I didn't. I was too busy being nasty, for which I'm sorry."

"I get it now. It's okay."

"It means heart. And so does Thaddeus. They both mean heart. I used to think we were one half of the same heart, that I'd never be whole without him. Now I know we are each whole. But I want to be with him again. I miss him."

"Goodbye, Lev. See you sometime, okay?"

"Sometime for sure, princess. And thanks." One foot hit the stair, then the other, and then it was fast. Partway up, they saw the pendant form. The pale silver metal formed first into one half of a heart, sliced cleanly down the center. It hung there for a second, then reformed itself into a whole heart. Then they saw it unlock and fall off into the ether. In a moment, it was gone. A second later, so was Lev.

There was a long silence, during which Carmen felt that mosquito feeling on her back again. The baby pendant had formed and unlocked, but hung there still. Now it was changing once more.

"Dulcie, look again. Back here! My pendant's changing! What's happening?"

Zeke was watching too, squinting at her back as if he couldn't believe what he was seeing. Dulcie's mouth fell open. "Oh, Carmen, this is too much! The baby is gone."

"Yes, yes…so what's there now?"

Zeke started to laugh, then Dulcie. Carmen leaned back helplessly, trying to see her own back.

"It's a thumbs up."

"A thumbs up? Like you mean…a thumb, pointing up? *That's* what's on my back now?"

"That's it, Carmen." He was still laughing.

What a cool place this is. A thumbs up.

"You're right, Carmen." Then he unfurled his massive wings, so that one surrounded Dulcie, and one Carmen.

"Let's go, song angels. Time to go home."

And so they did.

CPSIA information can be obtained
at www.ICGtesting.com
Printed in the USA
FFOW03n1902050418
46144974-47277FF

9 781634 929288